CW00868381

THE NEFARIOUS NECKLACE

A VEGAN VAMP MYSTERY

CATE LAWLEY

Copyright © 2017 Catherine G. Cobb
All rights reserved.

For Duke and Boone, who continue to provide me with at least as much laughter as sticky bloodhound drool

Lost Library Collection: Books 1-3

Witch's Diary

Lost Library Shorts Collection

The Covered Mirror: A Lost Library Halloween Short

Krampus Gone Wild: A Lost Library Christmas Short

SPIRELLI PARANORMAL INVESTIGATIONS

Spirelli Paranormal Investigations Season 1

Entombed: A Spirelli Investigations Novel

Writing as K.D. Baray

BEAUREGARD

Mistaken: A Seth Beauregard Short

BONUS CONTENT

Interested in bonus content for the Vegan Vamp series? Subscribe to my newsletter to receive a bonus chapter for *Adventures of a Vegan Vamp* as well as release announcements and other goodies! Sign up at http://eepurl.com/b6pNQP.

CONQUERING THE DOOR. OR THE BLOOD. MAYBE BOTH.

The door to the garage was innocuous enough.

It was an off-white color that was bright, but not startlingly so, and it was equipped with a generic, utilitarian doorknob. There was nothing inherently frightening or threatening about it. It was a pleasant, normal sort of door.

What was on the other side, however, made my skin crawl.

Commercial-grade refrigerators were meant to be filled with carrot juice and vegan shakes, not bottles of blood.

Granted, the sight and smell of blood didn't make me want to puke anymore, and that was a big improvement. But a fridge full of blood was still creepy. And gross. Every time I thought about that huge fridge of stasis-preserved human blood lurking sneakily in the shadows in my garage, I got the willies. As a vampire, that was downright embarrassing.

So here I was, standing in front of my own door, hesitating to enter my own garage—but trying to tackle the problem.

"Wembley!" I hollered.

If I couldn't get over my blood aversion, then I needed to have a chat with my vamp roomie about his blood-storage choices. It might be the coward's way out, but my garage shouldn't give me the willies. And there had to be a way to conquer my aversion besides living with the equivalent of a blood bank.

My phone chirped with my sometimes-partner Alex's ringtone. I gave the garage door a narrow-eyed look, then decided Society business should probably come first.

As a newly inducted member of the Society for the Study of Paranormal and Occult Phenomena—the local governing body for the magically enhanced community—and a contractor for the chief operating officer, Society calls hit the top of my priority list. And I was honest enough with myself to admit that working with Alex was fun.

I answered my phone on the second ring. "Hey, Alex. What's up?"

"I have a case for you."

I did a fist pump, then blushed when I saw Wembley had finally emerged from the back of the house and was watching me with interest.

Enthusiasm for my job was hardly a reason for embarrassment, but Wembley didn't help by smirking and saying, "Alex?"

I shrugged and then turned away from both Wembley and the garage door. A case was reason enough to celebrate, so I headed for the fridge and carrot juice. "You have excellent timing. I was about to have a chat with Wembley about his garage stash."

Wembley's discontented murmurings faded into the background as I ducked my head inside the fridge.

"Which stash is that? Food or equipment?"

Since I'd personally benefitted from Wembley's cache of

weapons, it would be more than a little hypocritical to complain about that particular stash. Tangwystl, a living sword with a surprisingly vocal thirst for blood, had been stored in that very same cache until she'd made her way into my hands.

"His food stash." And there were the heebie-jeebies again. If I could just get the skin crawling to stop, maybe I'd graduate to being an almost normal vampire. Who was I kidding? That wasn't going to happen.

"Ah." Alex paused then in a brisk tone said, "So about that case. Regular Society terms, your usual rate. Are you free?"

Alarm bells went off. No details, a phone call rather than a face-to-face visit... I smelled hinkiness. I set down the bottle of carrot juice on the kitchen counter. "What's the job? And who are we working for?"

"That's the beauty of this one. It would be your first solo assignment."

Since I was new to enhanced living and barely under-stood how the Society operated, I translated that to mean Alex didn't want to touch this particular case with a ten-foot pole. "Again—what's the job and who's the client?"

"Technically your client would be the Society, but Gladys—"

"Nope." I grabbed the juice and took a fortifying drink, thought about it, and then drained half the bottle. Gladys had that effect on me. Just thinking about working with her again had me comfort drinking.

"You don't even know what the case is. At least—"

I didn't hear the rest, because I hung up on him. Maybe that had been a tiny bit harsh? But Gladys... Nope. Not too harsh.

Gladys was lovely. I adored her. We'd always gotten

along well, and I'd even go so far as to call her a friend. Of a sort.

But taking her on as a client, even an almost client—nope. I'd already had Gladys as a client, twice over, and I had no desire to repeat the experience. Unless her life was on the line, I didn't want to have anything to do with the case.

And I would *not* feel badly about hanging up on Alex. If anyone could persuade me to do the unthinkable, it was Alex. He wasn't the type to use his powers for evil, but dumping Gladys on me was well within his moral code.

Abruptly ending the call was an act of self-preservation. I took a sip of carrot juice. While Gladys wasn't a physical threat, I had to consider my emotional well-being, too. I stared at the my carrot juice and hoped the guilt wouldn't last long.

The doorbell rang.

"Nuts." I flagged Wembley as he emerged for the second time from the back of the house. Boone, my recently adopted bloodhound, trailed sleepily behind him. "Don't answer that."

Persistent knocking ensued.

Wembley stood in the living room, obviously weighing who he wanted to piss off less. On the one hand, his roomie with the baby fangs and the bloodthirsty sword with the secret-not-so-secret crush on him. On the other, his older-than-dirt friend with mega-wattage wizard power and a sword that possessed no allegiance or opinions.

Wembley shrugged and shot me an apologetic look a split second before he headed to the front door.

In moments like these, I couldn't help thinking there wasn't much of the Berserker Viking left inside Wembley. *That* guy would have faced the wrath of Alex's sword just for the fun of it. Then again, that guy probably wouldn't be any fun to live with. It seemed there'd been a lot of anger and drugs involved with being a Berserker.

"I'll remember this the next time my mom and I chat," I called out from the kitchen. "Don't think I won't."

He didn't turn around, but he did briefly pause before he opened the door.

Ugh. Wembley and my mother. How had I let that happen? Then again, I hadn't really. Wembley had been a sneaky son of a gun and chatted her up on the phone when I wasn't around.

Alex walked in, greeted Wembley politely, then turned to me. "You have the manners of a belligerent teenager."

Boone sat down next to him and gave him a forlorn look until Alex rubbed his ears.

"Traitor," I said to the hound. Turning to Alex, I added, "No, I have manners. They're just absent when shady people try to manipulate me into doing unsavory things." I caught Wembley making a hasty exit down the hall to his bedroom and called after him, "I wasn't kidding. Chat, me and my mom. I won't forget, Wembley."

Alex's eyebrows rose. "Wow. He really is taking your mom out?" When I nodded, he added, "No wonder you're in a mood."

A mood? My eyes narrowed. At least Alex had the grace to look mildly regretful.

Boone sighed, looked at me, then Alex, sighed again, and then wandered away.

It was handy having a hound who understood human speech, especially when he sided with me. Giving up ear rubs was a pretty big deal for him and was a nice showing of solidarity. Granted, he was probably headed to wallow in my bed and spread his slobber generously on my duvet right now, but he'd still earned a little extra with dinner tonight.

"This mood I'm in is definitely telling me to pass on your case. But thanks for the offer." I gave him a look that made it clear I was not thankful.

"Look, I know Gladys can be challenging, but she has a legitimate complaint and none of the emergency response crew have time for this type of case. I'd look into it myself, but I'm otherwise occupied." Alex rubbed his neck. "Please? As a favor to emergency response."

Emergency response crew were a bizarre combo of paramedic, fireman, cop, and assassin. Since I could never be entirely certain they were coming to save and not exterminate me, they weren't my first choice to call in an emergency. And I wasn't particularly interested in doing any favors for them.

Alex, on the other hand, I'd always call him in an emergency. He had come through on more than one occasion, and he put others' safety—who was I kidding? *my* safety—above his own pretty regularly these days. That couldn't help but have an effect on a girl. Great. I owed him, and he was talking favors.

"If Gladys's complaint is legitimate, then why isn't the big boss man ordering one of you emergency response guys to investigate?" Seemed like a reasonable question to me, but Alex looked frustrated by it.

"The Society is stretched a little thin right now. You do recall that we recently lost our CEO?"

Of course I recalled. Hard to forget since his dead body had been buried in Gladys's new herb garden—while she'd thrown one of her Divorced Divas parties practically on top of the corpse. *That* was the kind of thing that happened when Gladys was involved.

I shook the image of the dead former CEO's naked dead body right out of my head. "I don't see the problem. You take over as acting COO, Cornelius acts as temporary CEO, and when a new CEO is voted in, Cornelius goes back to being the COO. Easy-peasy."

"Think about it, Mallory. Cornelius is more bureaucrat than politician, so he wants nothing to do with the executive position. The CEO was murdered, his assistant and wife executed for the crime. That makes continuity of leadership much more difficult. Unless Cornelius can pull a rabbit out of his hat, Texas might be looking at significant change in the near future."

"I gather from your tone that significant change means terrible things will happen."

"Blaine Waldrup and Oscar Hayes are the only candidates that Cornelius has found for the position." I didn't recognize the names, but Alex looked displeased. "There is also a segment of Society members who are using the current instability as an opportunity to test boundaries, which is in turn keeping emergency response busier than usual."

My head was starting to hurt. Emergency response was overtaxed, and I'd bet the normally efficient Cornelius was gonna have a heck of a time. "How is Cornelius supposed to find good candidates when the position pays the equivalent of a teacher's salary?"

"That's a generous estimate. I'd say more along the lines of a new teacher in an underfunded school district, maybe." Alex's jaw firmed. "The attraction isn't the money, and the problem isn't about finding candidates but finding the right candidate."

"So the lure is power and prestige and..." Words failed me, because I didn't get it. Alex had once explained the

Society in terms of a governing body, with the COO as the sheriff and the CEO as mayor. But CEOs were usually paid better than a poorly paid teacher, and where was this mysterious prestige?

Alex sighed. "Look. Austin is a hub of enhanced living, one of a few in the U.S. Each of the hubs concentrates power in its region."

"So controlling Austin is kind of a big deal?"

Alex crossed his arms. "Yes, it *kind of* is. Cornelius is doing his best to ensure that a reasonable candidate takes over the CEO position, one who will continue to modernize and give some consideration to humans, and that's consuming his time. He won't make a play for the position himself, unfortunately, and finding another remotely reasonable choice is proving difficult. Long story short, we're all *very busy*."

"Way to lay the guilt trip on, Alex." Worse, now I felt like a heel for hanging up on him. I finished off my carrot juice, screwed the cap on, and then made myself say the words. "Fine, I'll take the job. What's Gladys done now?"

"Maybe nothing. Gladys is the complainant, not the chief suspect this time." Alex's arms dropped to his side, and he frowned. "She claims her friend Bitsy has disappeared."

My ears perked up. "A missing person case?" Suddenly, Gladys didn't seem nearly the problem she'd been a few minutes ago. My very own missing person case! I blinked at the look on Alex's face and assumed a more serious mien. "Uh, I mean, that's unfortunate."

Getting my first solo case put me one step closer to sleuthing ninja status. Now, if I could just solve it, maybe I'd make it past baby ninja-in-training status.

2

A DIFFERENT SORT OF VAMPIRE

It turned out that Bitsy Jenkins *might* be missing. Or she could have done a runner. Or taken a vacay.

After Alex briefed me, I figured it was the uncertainty of the existence of a crime that got it assigned to me rather than the emergency response team's caseload. But I refused to let my enthusiasm wane.

As I drove to Gladys's house in the 'burbs, I considered the information I had.

Bitsy lived alone in an apartment in South Austin, not too far from both my house and the Society's headquarters. She worked as a waitress at a popular café and hadn't been to work the last three days. She was single and had no surviving family that she acknowledged. She was a newish vampire—whatever that meant. Being familiar with Alex's perception of time, that could mean she'd been transformed last month or a few years ago. Although Alex didn't have a timeline for her transformation, he did know that Gladys and Bitsy had met at a Society orientation. Since orientation was for the newly turned and the new to Austin, Bitsy was one or both of those.

I really needed to make one of those orientations. I'd missed the last one when the Society's CEO had shown up inconveniently dead in Gladys's bed. She was my life-coaching client at the time and, in her mind, I was the natural person to turn to in a crisis.

Attend orientation...or save Gladys from being executed for a crime I'd been pretty certain she hadn't committed? Unlike some vamps, I hadn't lost my moral compass when I'd been turned, so I'd opted for saving Gladys.

Since becoming a vampire, my life had acquired some unusual complications, and I hated to say that digging up the former CEO from Gladys's newly planted herb garden—where she'd "temporarily" stashed him—hadn't been the weirdest thing I'd ever done.

I pulled into Gladys's drive and couldn't help but admire the picture-perfect yard. Unlike many of her neighbors, Gladys did most of her own gardening. Whether it was the heat or just Texas culture, in my experience, most yardwork in the 'burbs seemed to be done by teenage children or yard services—not by women like Gladys.

Gladys's glorious head of bright red hair poked up above her well-groomed shrubs.

I waved as I climbed out of my Jeep.

Gladys gave me a brilliant smile. By the time I reached her, she'd removed her gardening gloves and extended a beautifully manicured hand. "Mallory, I'm so glad to see you. I can't believe the Society assigned you to the case." A brief flash of consternation passed across her face. "I thought Anton was going to chuck me out on my rear when I insisted on seeing his boss. And Cornelius, well, he didn't seem to take my concerns seriously." Her expression brightened. "It was Alex, wasn't it? He put in a good word for me, I'll bet."

Anton, or mean Mr. Clean, as I thought of him, was hardly a welcoming sort of guy, and he'd been a royal pain in my tush since day one of my vamp life. He put "killer" into the emergency response job description, literally. He was an assassin by magical classification. It wouldn't shock me if Anton had recommended quietly disappearing Gladys. If there was no Gladys, then there was no complaint and therefore no problem.

I really didn't like that guy.

"I'm not sure on the particulars, but I'm here now." I let go of her hand after a quick squeeze. I was developing the same dislike of shaking hands that permeated the enhanced crowd in Austin. "Do you have a few minutes to answer some questions?"

"Absolutely. Come inside." She gathered up her gloves and a huge pair of hedge trimmers. When she saw me eyeing the monster blades, she said, "Isn't being a vamp fabulous? I can work in the yard all day without getting burned. Or maybe I am getting a sunburn, and it's healing right away? Either way, it's heavenly."

I bit my tongue, nodded, and smiled. It didn't seem polite to comment that spending one's afterlife doing yard work seemed anything but heavenly. I'd briefly flirted with the idea of gardening after my transformation. I'd discovered my aversion to all things dirt, bug, and germ had practically disappeared, so why not garden? The impulse had lasted a whole two seconds, right until the reality of home ownership had sunk in. Houses were a lot of work.

I followed her inside, reminding myself that Gladys was due a little joy. Even if she found it in unusual places like gardening all day in the Texas heat.

She welcomed me into her kitchen and offered me a seat at the table. "Would you like a drink?"

"Ah, no. I think I'll pass." It seemed a wise choice, since the last time we'd discussed beverages she'd been rhapsodizing over her recently planted herbs and how they'd add a nice kick to some bloody concoction she planned to enjoy. My stomach rebelled, and it wasn't even the blood this time. Those herbs had been planted atop a corpse. Ick.

Some of my disgust must have shown, because Gladys gave me a sympathetic look and said, "Does b-l-o-o-d still make you sick?"

Because if it did, spelling the word would make everything better. I swallowed my smile. "That's actually getting a little better." I lifted my hand, cutting her off before she could offer me a blood-infused beverage. "I'm still not partaking."

A small crease appeared between her perfectly plucked eyebrows. "It's a shame, really. You'd feel so much better if you did, and you might not have all those—" Her eyes widened, and she pressed her lips together.

There was a missing woman to find—probably. I really should focus on that. But I couldn't resist. "What might I not have?"

"I shouldn't say." Her tone was firm, but I could see she was conflicted.

I leaned forward and lowered my voice. "You know, most of my exposure to enhanced living has been through the Society's emergency response unit, and they're light on vamps. And you know my roommate Wembley? He and I don't really talk about that kind of thing."

She blinked, her gorgeous, long lashes fluttering. "Yes, and he's a...*different* sort of vampire."

An uneasy feeling settled into the pit of my stomach, and this time it had absolutely nothing to do with blood or dead-guy herbs. Something about the way she'd said "different" had me on edge. Gladys hadn't been judgmental or cliquey in my previous experiences with her. Something was up, and if Wembley had been found wanting as a vamp, I could hardly be faring much better.

Most of my oddities and non-vampish quirks I'd kept to myself—primarily at Alex's urging—but not all of them. My aversion to blood and my stunted baby fangs, were two big ones I hadn't been able to hide.

When she didn't elaborate, I asked, "What makes you say that?" I asked the question with a friendly smile that I let inch up to my eyes.

"Oh, it's nothing." She clasped her hands together on the kitchen table. It was a careful, tidy gesture. Everything about Gladys had been careful and tidy before she'd been turned, before she'd divorced her husband…her bullying, control-freak husband.

I really thought she'd overcome the nasty ex and her unconventional vampire transformation. The Divorced Divas club that she'd started seemed like ample evidence of her recovery. She'd even started dating. And that thought triggered even more unease. I hoped her new beau didn't have anything to do with her recent shift in attitude.

Without uttering a word, I widened my eyes and gave her a confused look. With a little luck, and the pressure of absolute silence, maybe she'd spill the beans.

It took almost a minute of excruciatingly awkward silence before she caved. Her perfect posture drooped ever so slightly and she said, "Blaine doesn't think Wembley's a very good influence."

Bingo. The boyfriend, Blaine, *was* the bad seed. And if he didn't approve of Wembley, I didn't want to know what he had to say about poor little broken me. And that name, why did it sound so familiar?

"Blaine? That's the man you've been seeing?"

Her back straightened. "Yes, he's been so helpful. He's been a comfort amidst all of the changes I've been going through."

Apparently, I was chopped liver. It wasn't like I'd rescued her in Bits, Baubles, and Toadstools as she'd tried to consume mass quantities of fake blood, fangs hanging out for all the world to see. Oh, right—that *was* me.

With a saccharine smile pasted on my face, I said, "I'm so glad you've come this far. I remember when you couldn't be within twenty feet of a man without screaming bloody murder."

Gladys tipped her beautifully coiffed head and said, "Yes, it's difficult to have sex with a man if you can't be in the same room with one."

I inhaled so fast that I choked, and then I started to hiccup. Leave it to Gladys to be uniquely logical. I took a breath and held it, hoping the cure worked better for vamps than humans.

The woman had shrieked like a banshee when men approached her, not but a few weeks prior. Unlike my transformation, which was a complete blank thanks to a stout dose of roofies, Gladys retained bits and pieces of her transformation, and it had changed the way she saw men. Apparently, that hurdle was well and truly cleared. I clutched my side as the hiccups persisted.

That small crease appeared between her eyebrows again. "I don't think vampires are supposed to hiccup."

I dropped any attempt at superficial politeness, and, in between uncomfortable spasms, said, "This vampire hiccups."

The hiccups from hell that would never end were giving me a stitch in my side to rival the one I'd gotten when I'd attended spin class. The one time I'd attended spin class.

Gladys squinted—an odd sight, given vamps have exceptional sight—and said, "Are you crying?"

Nuts. The worst case of hiccups ever, because they were making my eyes water, and that was definitely something vamps didn't do. Tears were a big no-no, especially mine, since they tended to burn my face.

"No. Of course not." I looked at her like she was a crazy woman—then hopped up and excused myself to make an emergency phone call. Waving my phone, I said, "It's Alex. Important Society business. Be right back."

Then I booked it to her bathroom. I had to flush my eyes or I was going to end up with red streaks down my face, and then *that* secret non-vampish thing about me would be out. I swallowed a groan. There were so many these days.

I dried my face off, checked for signs of burn marks, and blew out a sigh of relief when there were none. I healed faster than my former human self, but those burns took a while to fade away.

After a quick inspection, I opted to powder my cheeks to hide any slight redness I'd missed. As I left the bathroom, I hovered for a second on the threshold. My hiccups had disappeared. The moment I'd been thinking of something else, they'd simply vanished. Some things hadn't changed when I'd become a vamp, and that was oddly comforting.

Gladys was seated at the kitchen table, but while I'd been in the bathroom, she'd retrieved a bottle of water for me. She gave me a worried look. "Is it Bitsy? Did they find her?"

"Ah, no." I slid into my seat. "But that's what I wanted to talk to you about. Why do you think Bitsy is missing?"

"But I don't think she's missing."

Uh-oh. I steeled myself for yet more of Gladys's brand of logic. "So, what exactly is the issue?"

Her eyes widened, and in a pleasantly confident voice, she said, "Oh, she's dead. I'm sure of it."

3

A MARY-LESS BLOODY MARY LUNCH

I considered Gladys a unique thinker. According to reliable sources—Alex and Wembley—the transformation from human to vamp always impacted the victim's personality. I believe the phrase "scrambled their brains" was used. In my case, many of the anxieties I used to deal with daily simply melted away. Many vampires sacrificed their empathy. I didn't have a clue what had happened to Wembley.

But Gladys didn't lack empathy—not exactly. And, so far as I knew, she hadn't been cured of some chemical imbalance. She was just a little...off.

If Alex were here, he'd kick me in the shin, a not-so-gentle reminder that upsetting Gladys would not aid the interview process. I opened the water bottle in front of me and took a drink. After I recapped it, I asked, "Did you tell Alex that Bitsy was dead?"

"No. Why would I tell Alex? I made my complaint to Anton."

It was like Gladys and my sleuthing buddy Bradley were sharing a brain. Bradley was all about details and accuracy.

"When you spoke with Anton, what did you tell him?"

"Oh, well, that Bitsy loved her job, but she hadn't been for three days. Four days, now."

Finally, a straight answer. I pulled a notebook and pen out of my purse. "What else?"

"That we had lunch plans on Saturday, and she hadn't shown."

I glanced up from my notepad. I hesitated to question what lunch for two vampires entailed, but the details might be important. "Lunch?"

She shrugged. "Two people meet at an agreed-upon time, typically around noon. It's a social event, sometimes with alcohol; you should maybe try it."

And, Gladys being Gladys, she actually meant exactly what she said. She wasn't giving me grief for my lack of social life, just wanted me to get out more.

"But two vampires? Meeting for lunch?" I started to tap my pen and stopped myself. Nervous fidgets were not the sign of a capable investigator, and I didn't have any evidence they'd been sipping *bloody* Bloody Marys. Or worse, the blood of *a* Mary. My stomach flip-flopped at the thought.

Gladys cocked her head. "You've gone all pale." And just a split second later... "Oh! No, not *that* kind of lunch. We meet for cocktails sometimes, but just cocktails. That was one of the things Bitsy missed from her human days: going to happy hour with the gals. She's new in the area and didn't have any girlfriends."

"So why lunch instead of happy hour?"

"Oh, well, that worked better for both of us. She worked evenings at the café, and I frequently have dinner plans with Blaine."

Blaine again. How had I not met this guy yet? *Focus, Mallory.* Blaine could wait. The missing woman less so.

Missing or dead woman. Pen poised over paper, I said, "So that's when you guessed that Bitsy was dead, when she failed to show for your lunch appointment."

"No."

I'd almost appreciate one of Alex's kicks in the shin, because it would mean that he also was hearing what I was hearing, suffering what I was suffering. "How about you tell me why you think Bitsy is dead and not just missing."

"She missed the monthly Divorced Divas meeting." Her eyes wide and innocent of any guile, she said, "Bitsy would never miss a Divorced Divas meeting."

"Of course she wouldn't." When Gladys just looked back at me with an agreeable expression, I said, "*Why* exactly wouldn't she?"

Gladys inched to the front of her chair. "She was interested in one of the attendees, Rosa Silver."

I shook my head. "She was interested in one of the women who attended your Divorced Divas meetings...and missing the most recent meeting—"

"On Monday."

"Missing the Monday meeting is why you think Bitsy is dead." Of course it was. I curbed my annoyance, because Gladys always made a certain kind of sense. I just had to sort through her responses for the logic that would be there...somewhere. "Exactly what do you mean by interested?"

"It's a secret, but given the circumstances—and I know I can trust you—I suppose it's okay to say. Bitsy was interviewing Rosa as a candidate for *transformation*." Gladys whispered the last word.

Secrecy made sense, because there were strict rules concerning transforming people into vampires. Rules I'd guess the missing Bitsy hadn't followed. Not to mention the pesky immunity issue. Most humans couldn't be transformed, because they carried a natural immunity to the virus.

My phone pinged with a text message, but I ignored it. "So she wasn't interested in Rosa romantically?"

"Oh, yes. They hooked up after the last Divas meeting. That's why Bitsy was so interested." Gladys's lashes fluttered. "Bitsy had a nice time."

"Bitsy met Rosa at your Divorced Divas meeting, liked her, had an intimate evening with her, and then decided she wanted to transform her?" It all seemed a little haphazard to me.

Being a vamp was a lifetime commitment—a vampire lifetime. That was nothing to sneeze at. And then there was all the rule-breaking that was happening. The Society's justice system was halfway stuck in the Dark Ages. I wouldn't want to run too far afoul of it, not without Alex about two feet away to make sure I didn't get beheaded or hung as a result.

Gladys blinked wide eyes at me. "Bitsy had a *very* nice time."

Okay, wild monkey sex. Good for them. But something was still odd about the whole thing. Becoming a vampire was kind of a big deal. "And what about immunity to the virus?"

"Bitsy got a blood sample." A small wrinkle appeared between Gladys eyes. "She was vague about the details." With a small shrug, Gladys said, "But however she managed it, she got the blood, had it tested, and found out that Rosa isn't immune. Bitsy received the lab results on Friday."

I stopped for a moment to consider the logistics of drawing your lover's blood with any kind of discretion. Nope, not seeing how that happened unless she'd been passed out. So—wild *marathon* monkey sex? I needed to give the question a pass for now, because I was finding it a little too distracting. And personal.

"Bitsy was extra excited to come to the meeting," Gladys said, "because she'd been looking for her first protégé since she arrived in Austin."

"Protégé?" That was a word I hadn't heard before. I knew that the neck raper who'd turned me was technically considered my progenitor, but "neck raper" worked better for me.

"You really don't know much about vampire society, do you?" She gave me a pitying look, as if my lack of knowledge somehow made me less. Less worthy? Less vampire? I wasn't sure what was going on in her head, only that she hadn't been the judgmental type, not in my past experiences with her. And she'd never expressed interest in the ins and outs of vampire society before.

I needed to meet this Blaine guy. And maybe kick him in his sensitive bits. Pretty sure it hurt vamps about as much as humans.

My phone pinged again. I removed it from my back jeans pocket and chucked it into my purse. A vibrating butt was one annoyance too far in this oddball interview.

"Let me just recap, Gladys." I glanced at the scribbles on the pad in front of me. Basically worthless, so I made additional, more legible, notes as I went along. "You're friends with Bitsy, good enough friends that she confided in you her desire to turn a human—to acquire a protégé." Gladys nodded, so I continued. "Even though she might have been breaking Society laws in doing that."

Gladys waited for me to continue, so I took that as an affirmation.

"When she didn't appear at your Divorced Divas

meeting on Monday, you grew concerned and reported her absence to emergency response, specifically to Anton, but you only told him Bitsy had missed lunch on Saturday and failed to show up to work for a few days."

She met my gaze and nodded earnestly. "That's correct —well, except I told him she was dead."

Anton must have verified that the woman hadn't been seen in a few days and modified Gladys's complaint to reflect that information. As much as I disliked the man, he was diligent.

The muffled sound of yet another text emerged from my bag. "And you didn't mention the Divorced Divas meeting or her reason for going because you didn't want to create any difficulties for Bitsy with the Society."

Gladys gave me a disappointed look. "Bitsy's dead. She certainly wouldn't mind, would she? I didn't want to involve Blaine. You know he's in the running to take over the CEO position?"

And that was why that name had sounded so familiar.

"Blaine would have been questioned because…"

She sighed, and I felt like the kid who couldn't quite keep up in class. Not a fair assessment of the situation. Not even a little bit.

"Blaine is much more pro-vampire than the current regime," she said. "I'm sure they'd assume that he influenced her."

"But he didn't."

"Of course he did. I just told you, he's pro-vampire. He's also very persuasive. And attractive." She tipped her head. "And so much better in bed than my ex."

Gladys in bed with Blaine, or any man so soon after her manic-man-hating phase, made my head spin. What little I knew of this Blaine guy was skeeving me out. He seemed to be taking advantage of Gladys, who had been a vulnerable mess not but a few weeks ago.

"Who's good in bed aside, do I understand you correctly that Blaine encouraged Bitsy to take on a protégé without the Society's knowledge, then she found a likely candidate, and then she disappeared—" Gladys's forehead creased, and I quickly backtracked. "Then you realized *Bitsy was dead.* Then you called emergency response, but left out everything to do with transforming a human."

"That's what I've been telling you."

And in a very Gladys-like way, she had. Unfortunately, when she'd passed along her concerns to emergency response, she'd left out all of the important parts. Of course they hadn't been concerned. Bitsy Jenkins was an adult. A full-grown *vamp.* The woman was allowed to take a vacay without telling her nearest and dearest. And from emergency response's perspective, the fact that Gladys was the source of the complaint made it inherently less reliable.

I reviewed my notes, making sure I'd captured all of the details and none of the Gladys crazy. On the second read-through, I figured that some of the crazy would have to stay, because it didn't make sense otherwise.

My phone rang, and it finally occurred to me that perhaps I hadn't suddenly become popular, and that Alex was trying—desperately—to get through to me. Who else would text and text? Bradley? Wembley? Actually, it could be any of the three of them. Nuts. I should have checked those messages.

I lifted a finger. "I apologize, but I need to get this."

I glanced at the caller ID and saw that it was Bradley. I swiped the screen.

Before I could speak, Bradley said, "It's Bradley."

"I'm in the middle of an interview, Bradley. Can it wait?"

"No. Alex won't stop texting me about you. Please call him back so he'll stop texting and calling me."

I apologized for the intrusion in his schedule—Bradley was big on schedules—and ended the call.

"Do you mind if I step outside for a minute, Gladys?"

"Of course. Feel free. Can I make you a fresh-squeezed lemonade?" As I dithered between it being too much trouble and oh so delicious, she delivered the foolproof Southern sales pitch: "I'm making some for myself, so it's no trouble at all."

"That would be lovely." And it would, because as far as I knew, there were no herbs in lemonade.

Once I was in the yard—well away from the infamous and now thriving herb garden—I called Alex.

"About time." He sounded more harried than normal.

"Seriously? You know I've been in an interview with Gladys." I lowered my voice to just a shade above a whisper. "It's not hard enough to get a straight story from her when my phone *isn't* going off every two seconds." Although...I could have shut the thing off.

"You could have turned it off." He made an annoyed sound. "I'm glad you didn't, though."

"What's the big emergency?"

"Didn't you check your texts? Never mind. There's been a murder."

And my mind leapt to the obvious conclusion: Bitsy. The missing woman was dead as Gladys had predicted. So Gladys wasn't completely whackadoo, which I'd already known, but was good to have periodically reinforced.

But then I remembered that the Society wasn't always very particular about the whys and wherefores of murder, so why all the frantic messaging? A dead guy in the world of the Society was more likely to produce a voicemail. Not even an urgent voicemail. More the kind that said, "Call me back when you get a chance."

"And the Society cares about this dead person more than usual, why?"

"The vic is the new assistant to the CEO."

Which was weird because we didn't have a CEO—oh, Cornelius, the interim CEO. Yeah, that made sense, sort of. "Oh, my, and we just lost the last one. Wait, I get why the Society would be concerned, but why are you so desperate to reach *me*?"

"*You* should care because the prime suspect is your missing woman, Bitsy Jenkins. The body was found in the trunk of her car."

Well, that was unfortunate.

4

THE GLADYS EQUATION

Gladys had just about convinced me that her vampy lunch buddy, Bitsy, was dead—which would have been convenient for Bitsy.

First the illegal transformation she'd been pursuing and now she was wrapped up in a murder investigation. If the Society decided to bring Bitsy in for either, then being dead was a great alibi and an even better escape plan.

I stretched the tense muscles in my neck. "Vampires get headaches. You know that, right?"

After a pause, Alex said, "Is that your way of telling me I'm giving you one?"

"Bingo, buddy." I started to pace alongside the back fence. "I might have some information for you. We need to meet."

"Yeah, I was afraid that Anton hadn't gotten the whole story. He doesn't have much patience for Gladys's type."

"Creatively logical?"

"Sure, that's a nicer way of saying it. How much longer before you're done there?"

"Twenty minutes?"

"Make it five. The dead woman, Tabitha Waters, was Becky Taylor's replacement. Her death is causing tension among the candidates."

"Explain to me again why the assistant to the CEP was replaced before the actual CEO?"

"An assistant is hired; the Society's CEO is selected. You've got four minutes." And then he hung up.

This case might be wrecking my attempts at inner joy. I would not let work—or Alex—put a crimp in my happy. I'd already had that life, dumped it, and gotten a new and improved version. I was not going back.

I marched into Gladys's house, ready to drink my lemonade and finish her interview, however long it took.

She met me at the door with my purse in one hand and a cute pink to-go cup in the other. "I just turned on my phone and got the news. Tabitha Waters is dead." She handed me my purse then the drink. "You have to explain to Alex that it couldn't have been Bitsy, because she's dead. And you have to prove that Blaine didn't do it, so that he can still have his nomination confirmed on Friday."

I looked at the drink—who had to-go cups in their kitchen?—and then at my purse.

"I tucked your notes inside your purse."

"Thank you." I shifted the strap higher on my shoulder. "You know that I haven't been assigned to Tabitha's case?"

Gladys gestured to the living room, the next room over on the way to the front door. I was being hustled out the door. "You weren't assigned to my case when I came under suspicion for murder, and you still kept the Society from hanging me with one of those special vamp-killing ropes."

She wasn't wrong, and yet it was not quite applicable here. I tried to point this out, in a gentle way. "But you didn't kill Dyson; someone else did."

She put her hand on my back and urged me toward the front door. "Exactly. Bitsy and Blaine didn't kill Tabitha, so it's basically the same."

"Not the same, Gladys. Not at all the same."

But she wasn't listening, or she was ignoring the parts she didn't want to hear. She opened the front door and said, "You're the only detective I trust to find the killer. The real killer. I know Bitsy and Blaine are innocent."

A rush of pride mingled with exasperation. It was pretty cool that Gladys thought of me as a detective. I had been doing more work for the Society, and I was enjoying the work—as a contractor. No way I'd join emergency response.

I sighed. "I'll do what I can to find Tabitha's killer and to locate Bitsy."

"Bitsy's—"

"I know, Gladys. You're convinced that Bitsy's dead. But without evidence to the contrary, I have to work on the assumption that she's still alive. That means finding Bitsy alive or conclusive evidence to the contrary."

Gladys cocked her head and, after a second or two, nodded. "You do what you have to, so long as you clear Bitsy and Blaine. Since they're both innocent, that shouldn't be hard—and then you just have to convince the Society."

She couldn't see past the innocence of two people she'd only just met. She hadn't been so trusting when I'd entered her life. It was like her reserve, her previous hurts, had been washed away. I examined her more closely.

Maybe she'd been brainwashed.

"What's wrong?" she asked, startling me out of my rather rude examination.

I stepped back. "Sorry. Just thinking. I'll be in touch if I have more questions about Bitsy."

By the time I climbed into the Grand Cherokee, I was

half convinced someone had been messing with Gladys's head. I stared at her garage door, trying to figure out why. And who. Blaine? Bitsy?

I shook my head and started the car. Alex was going to start calling me again if I didn't show up on time, or—worse yet—I might miss out on some of the juicy detective stuff.

As I followed my phone's navigation to the address Alex texted me, I considered alternatives to explain Gladys's persistent faith in Blaine and Bitsy's innocence.

Maybe she'd relapsed and latched on to the nearest available support. She'd bounced from an abusive relationship with her ex-husband to a life of independence prematurely ended by a violent attack. Except she hadn't died from those injuries; she'd become a vampire. That was a lot of stress, a lot of change, and a lot of bad luck in a short period of time.

Or maybe she was a victim of manipulation. She'd be a prime target after everything that had happened to her. Users and abusers seemed to have a sixth sense when it came to sniffing out the vulnerable.

Or maybe she was in love. That always did strange things to a person.

An image of a certain hot APD detective popped into my head, which made me add lust to the list. Love or lust, they both made people crazy.

Detective Gabe Ruiz was certainly making me a little crazy. Our first date was supposed to have been last weekend, but he'd rescheduled when something at work "blew up." Metaphorically, thank goodness. I'd freaked out, and he —thankfully—thought my literal-mindedness was funny. But was it such a stretch that things might go boom at a police station? Not when vampires sucked blood around every other corner and golems stole body parts to create their offspring. That stuff was real. The world was a weird and creepy place. Bombs seemed almost normal in comparison...almost.

The driver behind me honked his horn, and I looked up to find the stoplight had changed to green. Probably best not to think about Gabe or the oddities of enhanced living when I was en route to the scene of a murder. Better to focus on driving. Unlike Alex, my rocking reflexes only popped up in times of extreme stress, and Austin traffic wasn't quite *that* bad.

I hadn't previewed the route when I'd entered it into my navigation program, so I was a little surprised to find myself just around the corner from my house in southeast Austin. My house *and* Society headquarters.

My navigation routed me past the Society's retail storefront, Bits, Baubles, and Toadstools, and then down a heavily shaded street which housed several hotels.

Police lights flashed in the parking lot of one of the smaller hotels. I glanced at the map on my phone, and darned if that wasn't my destination.

Spiffy. Just fantabulous. A dead body was one thing. I'd been dealing with bodies left and right since I turned all vampy. But the cops? Paranormal and the police did not mix well.

Not in an official capacity, anyway. Unofficially, I was hoping for better. Because the dishy Detective Ruiz, homicide detective and very dedicated cop, had a date with this very paranormal gal, and I was thinking we'd mix just fine.

5

DAISIES, DATES, AND DEAD BODIES

I pulled into the lot and parked in a far corner, away from the flashing lights. Time enough for me to consider the ramifications of cop-vamp relationships after I made it through this particular fiasco.

Tabitha couldn't have just died quietly and unobtrusively, could she?

If Bitsy—or whoever—had not only killed Tabitha but also intentionally left her body to be discovered by any passing human, Cornelius and his tidy bureaucratic sensibilities were going to have a conniption. The only thing worse would be some overt indication that the enhanced community was involved. But surely no one could be that careless?

As soon as the thought entered my head, I felt a distinct sense of foreboding. My dubious precognition skills at work? Hopefully not.

I pulled my phone out of my pocket and called Alex. He answered on the first ring.

"Where are you? I'm parked in the northeast corner of the parking lot, and I don't see you or your car."

"I'm driving my personal vehicle today." Alex's voice disappeared, replaced by muffled, unintelligible noises.

"Alex." When he didn't reply, my heart rate cranked up. "Alex? Are you okay? Alex!"

"Calm down. I'm fine." After a slight hesitation, he said, "Panic attacks are imaginary, remember?"

I snorted in response as I exited my car. He and I both knew that I defied the vamp norm, and that I had retained some very human characteristics, including physical responses to stress that were atypical for vamps. And I was allowed to get a little worried about the guy. He had a knack for endangering himself while protecting others, an endearing and yet nerve-racking trait.

"I'm in the back of a police cruiser. I'd appreciate it if you had a chat with Detective Ruiz and convinced him to release me."

I swallowed a groan as I locked my car. The detective and I had a rescheduled date coming up in a few days—our first. So we were in that awkward "about to go out but hadn't yet" place. What better time to hit him up for a favor?

"I'm heading toward the crime scene now. Are you a suspect?"

Which was just a ridiculous thought. Sure, Alex killed people, but he didn't *murder* them. And he only killed people when they refused to be apprehended and processed through the Society's justice system.

"I don't think so, but they've already questioned me and taken my contact information, and I'm still here."

I picked up my pace and made a beeline for the flashing lights. There was an ambulance with a young woman in the back receiving oxygen, a handful of squad cars, and two unmarked cars, one of which was Gabe's.

A uniformed officer intercepted me well before I

reached the squad cars. "This area is closed to the public, ma'am."

A familiar dark head emerged from the crowd and turned in my direction. I bounced on my tiptoes and waved. Even from this distance, I could see Gabe's amused exasperation.

The cop who'd intercepted me—Officer Perez, according to his nametag—looked warily over his shoulder.

Gabe waved me through, but Officer Perez said, "Just a minute. I need your name and contact information."

After he jotted down the time and my details in a little notepad, he let me pass, but didn't look particularly happy about it.

Gabe knew what I was, and generally about the Society, but he wasn't in on all the details. Not yet. So I needed to keep the Society as far from his investigation as possible. He'd had a week to decide if he was in or out, and had requested more time. Being *in* meant knowing things that no one else did—and keeping those secrets. Being *out* meant having a portion of his memory wiped. I wasn't entirely sure the witches doing the memory excision would be using the magical equivalent of a scalpel. I was thinking more along the lines of a hatchet.

I hoped I didn't find out.

Gabe met me halfway and, very quietly, said, "Victim has two punctures on her neck. No cause of death yet, but from her pallor I'd say she lost a lot of blood."

"Oh." That was bad. Really bad.

No, wait, that was weird. Vamp saliva healed puncture wounds. Also, vamps drank *human* blood, and Tabitha was anything but human if she'd been the new assistant to the Society's CEO.

Catching sight of a muscle tic in Gabe's jaw, I came back around to really bad.

"Nothing else to say?" he asked.

I gave him a sheepish look. "Alex isn't a vampire?"

Gabe shook his head. "Alex showed up well after the body was found, and he had a scheduled appointment with Tabitha five minutes after his arrival time, confirmed by her appointment book. As long as the security tape we're pulling doesn't have him stashing the body in the trunk, he should be fine." Gabe narrowed his eyes. "It won't, will it?"

"No!" I lowered my voice. "No, of course not. I told you, he's not even a vampire. And before you get any funny ideas, I can't drink blood, remember?"

Gabe just frowned in response.

"You know, it's possible her death isn't related to the Society."

Gabe rubbed the stubble on his chin. "Really? Was the victim not a member?" I pressed my lips together, and he continued, "And the victim was found in the trunk of Bitsy Jenkins's car. Was Bitsy not a member?"

Those were probably all rhetorical questions, so I did the polite thing and refrained from answering. I wasn't sure how to look sweetly innocent, but I gave it my all with wide eyes and pouty lips. "Any chance I can see the victim?"

Gabe's eyebrows rose and his lips tightened. I was pretty sure if we'd been anywhere but on the edge of a crime scene, he'd have busted out laughing.

I gave up on my inadequate display of sweet innocence. "Fine. Probably too much to hope for."

"Way too much," he said. "But I wouldn't have missed the effort for anything. Kind of a cross between bewildered puppy and a cartoon fish."

"What's this look telling you?"

Gabe cleared his throat. "Shut up or I'm not getting that dinner date no matter how many flowers I send you."

"Smart man."

"But you liked the flowers?"

I grinned at him. "I adored the flowers." Three bouquets so far: an autumn arrangement when he'd asked me out, a perky pink and white daisy arrangement when he'd canceled—to cheer me up—and he'd gone traditional when he rescheduled, with a dozen red roses.

Wembley had approved, and that was no small standard to meet. Wembley had an eye for color and design that he'd, oddly enough, picked up between fighting in various conflicts across the globe. He hadn't even turned his nose up at what he'd called clichéd red roses, because they'd been particularly fine.

Gabe looked over my shoulder and nodded at someone in the distance. "Alex is about to be released. Think you can keep an eye on him? Keep him out of trouble?"

Now I was the one about ready to bust out and laugh. Like I could control Alex. "I'll stick to him like glue. Promise."

"But not so close that you and I can't have that dinner tomorrow night, I hope."

And just my luck, that was when Alex joined us. Not that I was hiding the fact that Gabe and I had plans; it just hadn't come up. And it wouldn't have ever come up if Alex would ask me out. But he hadn't, and Gabe had. And I really liked Gabe.

The two men nodded a greeting.

"You bailing me out, Mallory?" Alex asked.

"Nah," I said. "They're just done with you."

Gabe removed a small pad and pen from his breast pocket, opened it, and made a few notes. "I need you to answer a few questions, since I'm technically interviewing you now. What's the connection between you and Tabitha Waters?"

"I didn't know her."

"But Tabitha is a member of the same paranormal society as Mallory and I." Alex shifted closer to me. He'd done that before with Gabe, gotten all weirdly proprietary. Weird, because Alex and I weren't an item. On-again, off-again partners with shared secrets, but definitely not an item. I could be interested—who was I kidding? I totally was, but then *he* hadn't seemed interested, and then Gabe asked me out... I sighed. Alex was complicated.

"Mallory?" Gabe said.

"Sorry." I focused on the here and now. "Long story short, I'm sure I would have met her eventually, but as it is, I didn't even know her name until this morning."

Gabe made a note and then asked, "And Bitsy Jenkins? Are you familiar with her?"

"Familiar, yes. We have a mutual acquaintance, but I've never met her either." I met Gabe's yummy, warm brown eyes, and asked, "Is that good for now? You have my details, and we can always get together later to discuss it further."

No sooner had Gabe released us than Alex turned on his heel and left. I shot Gabe an apologetic look and hurried after Alex.

When I caught up, I noticed we were heading to my Grand Cherokee. I looked around to make sure I wasn't accidentally sharing his super secret, then asked, "So, what do the local spooks have to say?"

"Spirits. They're not the same as ghosts—which is what I assume you mean when you say spook?" Alex held out his hand for my keys.

That was one of our things. He had control issues and

wicked reflexes, so he always drove regardless of whose car we were in.

I dug the keys out of my jeans pocket and chucked them at him. "Okay, what do the spirits have to say? Surely there were some floating around this area."

He nodded and unlocked the car. "A person, identity unknown but in manly clothing." He caught my gaze and shrugged. "Spirits aren't always good with details or all that cooperative. It just depends on which ones happen to be in the area. This manly clothing-wearing person drove Bitsy's car to the lot this morning, went inside the hotel, and returned with a body. Get this, he then *left and came back*, parked, popped the trunk, and walked away."

Alex got in the car, so I hurried around the front and got in. "How are you not excited? That has to be the killer. Bam, a big clue right off the bat." I had to restrain myself from doing a happy dance. Partly because Bitsy didn't appear to be the killer—not if manly clothes meant a man—and that meant one of Gladys's buddies was in the clear. Also, I loved clues.

"More than one clue, several clues. Possibly a man— we'll call the 'manly clothing' clue more evidence for a male perpetrator than against. A perpetrator who wanted the body for some reason but also wanted Tabitha found without risking returning her to her room. But we still have no idea who that man was and no idea who killed Tabitha. Our driver could have simply been part of a body disposal gone wrong."

"Oh, but there's video. If the video cleared you, then it has to have a clue as to the real killer—or the body dumper."

"Not if our manly clothing-wearing person masked himself from the camera."

I'd forgotten about that. It had come up in a previous case, my first case. "Is it only vampires who have that ability?"

"Anyone with skill in illusion and witches. And if a witch can do it—"

"Anyone can buy it." I sank down in my seat. That was just disappointing. Not that I hadn't benefitted from witch services myself, but it was disheartening to see our suspect pool grow so quickly.

"You're learning. So give me a recap of what we do know, without the wild leaps to unrealistic and unprovable conclusions. We've got twenty minutes of road time to fill."

"Wait, where are we going?"

"To interview another suspect, Blaine Waldrup."

I didn't have any proof that Bitsy was dead, and the evidence we *did* have not only failed to conclusively prove her innocence but it also wasn't something we could openly share. Alex's spirit sources were very much on the downlow. And now we were off to interrogate Blaine and treat him like the suspect he was. Gladys wouldn't be pleased.

I began to envision what it might look like to have Gladys as an enemy. It didn't seem like a good idea.

6

BABY FANGS STRIKE AGAIN

I'd just finished recapping what Alex and I knew—not very much—when some serious holes emerged.

Since Alex had told me he was on a case this morning, I'd been assuming the case was Tabitha's—but that didn't fit. "How did you find out about Tabitha's murder?"

"I drove into a parking lot filled with cops," Alex said.

"You said you were on another case and that was why you couldn't handle Gladys's. Was Tabitha a part of the other case?"

"I'm technically on a few cases now, but Tabitha was helping me with one you're already familiar with. I've been trying to track down the rest of the stones." Alex shot me a quick look, then turned his attention back to the road. "You remember, the amethyst necklace that was disassembled."

Of course. I'd forgotten about the infamous Bethia Belleau, succubus extraordinaire, mistress to the rich and famous, and owner of a fabulous amethyst necklace. At least, she had been back in the eighteen hundreds.

"Yeah that might have slipped my mind in the bustle of winding up that last case."

"And dating." He didn't look particularly concerned by the fact. And yet he'd mentioned it.

"We haven't actually made it to the first date yet, but, yes, I've had a lot on my mind. What does Tabitha have to do with the missing stones?"

"She was a succubus."

After I picked my jaw up off the ground, I said, "I'm sorry—what?"

His lips twitched. "Don't sound so shocked. How is she any different from a vampire?"

"Uh, death. Killing people makes her different."

"And there you go, making assumptions. Vampires have learned to sip to survive and have found alternatives to drinking from the source. Tabitha did the same." He grinned and took a deep breath. "You should have seen her burlesque show. And the sex…"

"Ugh. Is there anyone you haven't slept with in the Society?"

His eyes met mine. "You." But then he turned his gaze to the road and my heart started beating again. "And I never had sex with her. Sex that depletes me physically doesn't suit my particular lifestyle. The fact that succubi are fabulous in bed is a universal truth. Tabitha had a number of partners, in keeping with the 'sip rather than gorge' lifestyle, and I doubt you'd hear any complaints about the recovery period."

Ick. Ick, ick, ick.

"Maybe if I had to drink blood to survive I'd get it, but I don't. It sounds disturbing on a very personal level."

"You just have to think of sex as food."

I tried—and failed. "Nope. That's not working for me."

"But for the grace of magic or DNA, or whatever it is that caused you blood aversion, go you."

As usual, he made a good point. Sometimes Alex was a nicer person than me. Not that anyone else would agree, but I knew. "Fine, I'll try not to get all judgy and holier than thou."

"So big of you."

I wasn't trying to sound like a condescending twit, and yet... "Sorry. Really."

He shrugged.

"Did she at least give you some good info, before...you know? Oh! And if she's a succubus, can a vamp even drink her blood? I know vamps can't drink vamp blood."

"Vamps can drink succubus blood, witch blood, wizard blood, but not vamp because of the virus it carries, and not golem because they're no longer alive. It's my understanding that anything but human is less palatable and fails to meet a vampire's complete dietary needs."

Speaking of ick. All that talk of blood gave me a case of the creepy skin crawlies, but no nausea. Yay for me.

"You okay?" Alex asked. "You're looking a little pale. I thought you were getting better. And what about your obsession with Wembley's garage stash? Are you sure your blood aversion isn't getting worse?"

"Hey, at least the upholstery isn't plastered with..." I struggled to remember the last thing I'd eaten. "Ooooh. I might be hungry."

And the more I thought about it, the hungrier I was. The slight, symmetrical pressure on my bottom lip could only mean one thing.

"Put the baby fangs away." He glanced at me and then chuckled. "They still haven't gotten any bigger."

I would have said something snarky, but I hadn't quite mastered speech while fanged, so I refrained. I dug in my purse hoping against reason I'd remembered to stash a bottle of veggie juice or a vegan shake. Something to take the edge off and make my fangs go away.

"Try the glove compartment."

I know I didn't stash goodies in my glove compartment; I'd have remembered that.

"Go on," Alex said. "Wembley probably has a few bottles tucked away in the car somewhere, and that's where I'd start."

I popped open the glove compartment to find, wonder of wonders, a bottle of my favorite drink: spicy veggie juice. And none of that low-sodium nonsense. I'd determined through trial and error that this vegan vamp needed her sodium.

I downed half the bottle, not the easiest of tasks with fangs protruding—even baby ones. But then they receded. I could feel the lack of pressure on my lower lip.

"You know what this means, right?" Alex asked.

"That Wembley is a stand-up guy?"

Alex tilted his head. "Yes, but more than that. He cooks for you. He stocks your car with an emergency stash of food. He's like your vamp mom."

I knew where he was going. "Ugh. You're right." I sighed, perhaps a little dramatically. "I need to get over the blood in the garage. I shouldn't inconvenience my roommate—"

"The best roommate you could possibly have."

"Right, rub that in. But I do understand. I shouldn't make getting his regular blood fix any harder just because I'm a little squeamish. But, hey, we might have unraveled another piece of my vampire puzzle. My fang display coinciding with a missed meal or two does make me wonder if I'm more susceptible when I'm hungry."

"If you'd keep yourself well fed, that might solve more

than a few problems, including your unpredictable fang flashing."

He was right—but that required planning and preparation, not two of my strengths since I'd been turned. Prevamp me would have been on top of it, but vamp me found keeping a closet full of clean clothes and feeding my hound challenging enough in the planning department.

I swallowed another mouthful of juice. Being hungry sucked, so it seemed an easy enough choice. "I'll try to eat better. You know, if Wembley's my vamp mom, you're like my paranormal pop."

Alex winced. "I'll pretend I didn't hear that. So what other unanswered questions are boiling in that brain of yours?"

"Actually, now that I think on it, how did Gladys know that Tabitha had been killed? I'm sure she checked her voicemail messages when I went outside to call you. But who called to tell her?"

"Information in the Society spreads much like gossip in a small town. It could have been anyone."

I thought back to the timeline. "Could it, though? This looks like someone knew about Tabitha's death before you. There's a pretty narrow window of time when the mystery caller could have telephoned Gladys. I arrived around ten, and that's probably when Gladys would have shut her phone off."

"And I finally reached you via Bradley a little after ten thirty. One option is someone who was at the crime scene when I was there: a bunch of human cops, the witness who saw the trunk was partially open and looked inside—also human—and human paramedics."

I looked out the window to find that we'd left the city.

We were in the boonies. "So either a human contacted Gladys for some unfathomable reason or the killer did. But why? What possible good could that do him?"

"If it was Blaine, it could be as simple as damage control." He altered the pitch of his voice. "I need your help, honey. I wasn't involved with Tabitha's murder, but they'll suspect me. Convince your friend to prove me innocent." Alex turned off the main road onto a country road.

I rubbed my forehead. "It just seems so far-fetched. Then again, if you're right, we're headed to a killer's house."

The Grand Cherokee started to bounce and vibrate as the paved road gave way to gravel.

"Don't worry. There's two of us and only one of him."

"You're not making me feel any better. Tangwystl!" I called my sword to me, a nifty trick I'd discovered a few weeks before. And just like the excellent little magical sword she was, she appeared in my right hand. I would never get tired of that trick. Especially since it was really hard to remember to bring a sword when you weren't used to carrying one.

"You're going into our interview armed with a blade?"

I glared at him. "Aren't you?"

"Sure, but mine's hidden."

Nuts. He had me there. I'd have to figure out how to hide her. I knew she could do it, because Wembley had complained about the decade or two when she'd gone missing—except she hadn't. She'd been hiding from him in a fit of pique over his perceived neglect. My sword had a little crush on Wembley.

"Fine. I'll leave her in the car. I can always holler for her if we get in a tight spot." I petted her grip and whispered an apology. She grumbled—something about blood, I'm sure—and then was silent.

Alex raised his eyebrows, but did not comment on the unlikelihood of me saving the day with a sword when he was around to do it ten times better. Maybe a hundred.

I blew a raspberry at him, but only because Tangwystl thought I should.

7

USED CAR SALESMEN NUMBERS ONE AND TWO

A lex pulled off the gravel road and onto a paved drive. A very long drive.

"Have you asked Bradley to pull information on Tabitha, Bitsy, and this Blaine guy?" I pulled out my phone, ready to text the master of cyber-research.

"I haven't, and you won't. These aren't humans, Mallory. He shouldn't be digging into their covers online. Not yet, and not unless we can give him a targeted search. But have him pull the police report, if he can. I doubt it will have any new information, but better to check. And if he can get that girl's name, the witness who found Tabitha's body, then have him pull a full background on her." After a brief hesitation, he said, "And Gladys's calls, incoming and outgoing, this morning."

I tapped away on my phone as he spoke. I wasn't keen on digging into Gladys's phone records, and I had to remind myself that she wasn't the client; she was the complainant. The Society was paying me. And then there was the simple fact that the truth mattered, even if it wasn't something I wanted to hear.

I ended the text with *xoxoxo*, mainly because I knew it would drive Bradley a little nutty, and I was in that kind of mood. "And done."

"Good, because we're here."

And were we ever. The place was huge. It looked like a colonial mansion, a little bizarre in the middle of Central Texas. Cooling the place alone had to be the equivalent of a monthly mortgage payment for a house in my neighborhood.

"Not sure how you can look so shocked," Alex said. "You didn't even see the golf course on the way in."

"I'll try to tone down my incredulity long enough to meet this guy, but I was already not liking him. A personal golf course in a place that suffers intermittent drought is not cool. Am I crazy or is that reason enough to find him guilty?"

Alex's lips twitched. "I remember a time not so long ago when you criticized the Society's lack of due process. Are you telling me that your due process concerns wane when they're in conflict with your personal agenda?"

I threw open my door. "Central Texas drought, private golf course." I ticked them off on my fingers. "Two reasons I'm allowed to be judgy."

Alex got out of the car and closed his door much more quietly than I had mine. "Come on. I bet they spotted us coming from halfway up the drive."

And he was right. The front door opened before Alex lifted his hand to ring the bell.

And that was when I met used car salesman number one and his smarmy competitor, used car salesman number two.

Except they weren't used car salesman; one of them was a candidate for the Society's CEO position.

After ushering us into his massive entryway, number one extended his hand to Alex. "Blaine Waldrup. Alex Valois, if I'm not mistaken?"

Alex nodded and only briefly hesitated before shaking Blaine's hand. Odd. I'd have thought a guy with political aspirations would know better than to shake hands. Or maybe it was a test. But if it was, had Alex just passed or failed?

Blaine turned expectantly in my direction.

Alex introduced me as his colleague, which was a pleasant surprise. When Blaine heard my name, his demeanor shifted subtly. I might not have otherwise noticed, but my meeting with Gladys had armed me with a little insight into CEO candidate Blaine Waldrup. He didn't like different, and he didn't think much of me.

I smiled pleasantly at him and didn't offer my hand.

He was old enough to practice an earlier generation's custom of allowing the lady to determine if shaking hands was appropriate, so I skated by without having to touch him. Although, looking at his perfectly coiffed blond hair and expensive suit, I might be mistaken. He may simply have wanted to avoid touching me.

Blaine turned to the man standing next to him, a muted, less obvious version of himself. Light brown hair rather than blond, a few inches shorter, and a smile that at least pretended to be genuine and didn't blind me with overly bright veneers. "May I present Oscar Hayes, another candidate for Dyson's position."

Oscar nodded at Alex and said, "Good to see you again. Ms. Andrews, a pleasure." Alex and I murmured appropriate responses. "Blaine and I were sharing a friendly competitors lunch when we heard the news. Terrible business."

And he meant it. I could *feel* that he truly thought it was all a terrible business. But what the heck was a friendly competitors lunch? And if they'd shared a meal, at least one of them was probably eating real food. It looked like Mr. Hayes wasn't a vampire. Too bad it was beyond rude to ask what exactly he was.

But I could ask about his politics.

I let my curiosity loose and said, "I'm new to the community, Mr. Hayes, and this is my first selection. I'm not sure of the protocol, but can one ask about a candidate's platform?"

Oscar gave me a politician's smooth smile, designed both to put me at ease and to assure me of his absolute competence. "I'm less of a traditionalist than Blaine, more interested in maintaining the status quo."

So, in other words, no, one did not ask. I nodded amiably, as if he'd actually provided me with some useful insight into his politics.

Blaine wasn't nearly so diplomatic. "Ms. Andrews, what you fail to understand is that the Society is not a democracy or even a republic. We tend more toward the oligarchical model." And just in case I didn't understand his already plain speech, he added, "You have no vote."

"That doesn't preclude curiosity, does it?" I thought that was a rather tame response.

Alex might have disagreed, because he quickly interceded before Blaine could respond. "I've recently received a nomination, so I'm sure you'll want to include me in the next friendly competitors lunch."

He was kidding, right? I checked to see if he'd give me a wink-wink kinda look. And I had to work to keep my jaw from dropping. No wink-wink. No nudge-nudge. How did he not tell me before now that he was in the running for his boss's *boss's* position. I'd call that relevant info.

"Ah, yes." Oscar nodded approvingly. "So you've decided to accept the nomination. Excellent choice. Excellent."

Once I'd mustered a more appropriately neutral look—I hoped—I saw that Blaine wasn't nearly so pleased as Oscar. He managed a weak smile, then turned to Oscar. "Perhaps you'd prefer to stay, Oscar? Have another drink, a congratulatory one, with my guests?"

"I'm afraid not. As I mentioned earlier, I've got some family business to attend to in town this afternoon, and I have to run home first." Oscar glanced at his watch. "It's a pretty good drive up north from here." Addressing Alex and me, he added, "I live in Round Rock these days."

An Austin Society politician living in the 'burbs. That was unexpected.

Alex stepped to the side as Blaine escorted Oscar to the door, he said, "I'll be in touch. We have a few questions for you as well."

"Yes, of course." Oscar pulled out a card case and presented both Alex and me with a business card. Then he nodded at Blaine, thanked him again for an excellent lunch, and left.

That left his slimy, more obnoxious counterpart to entertain us. Good times. I couldn't help but feel the future of the Society was looking grim if Blaine was in the mix. Silver lining: if he did kill Tabitha, he probably wouldn't be leading the Society into a vampire revolution. But then again, I'd be dead, because Gladys would have murdered me.

I sighed, then followed our host through his ostentatious marble entryway. Since Blaine had his back to us briefly, I mouthed, "What is Oscar?"

Either he could read minds or lips, because he actually understood enough to reply, "Coyote."

That solved the lunch question. Meat and more meat, not just Bloody Marys and blood-spiked cocktails.

Blaine directed us to a study near the front of the house. When a pretty petite woman in a maid's uniform came by to see if we needed anything, his expression turned sour. "Where have you been, Rosa? I had to serve my lunch guest myself." He must have realized that berating one's staff in front of guests, even uninvited ones, was less than appropriate, because he said, "Never mind. I won't be needing you further this afternoon."

So much for those congratulatory drinks.

He must have decided Alex and I didn't rate high enough on the social scale to merit refreshments. I'd be surprised if a place with its own golf course didn't have more than one in-home staff person. But then again, this was no normal home. How did it work when the homeowner was a vampire? Only enhanced persons need apply? Or were humans good enough to work in service to the snobbish Blaine Waldrup?

Oh, what fun this interview would be. I could already feel the need for a shower coming on.

8

BED, BITE, AND BYE

"Please, have a seat." Blaine gestured expansively, leaving the choice to us. Once I'd settled into an armchair and Alex was perched on the edge of an uncomfortable-looking sofa, Blaine said, "So how exactly can I help you?"

His smile was so fake it made my eyes hurt. Or maybe it was the brightness of his veneers.

Per his usual, Alex didn't take notes, he simply started asking questions. "When did you discover Tabitha had been killed?"

"I thought that was clear. Not until you contacted me during lunch to make this appointment. It came as a complete surprise to me."

I tried to keep a straight face as he spouted the blatant lie.

"You haven't spoken with Gladys?" I asked. "Or texted with her?"

"No, not today. Should I be concerned?" He made sustained direct eye contact with me for the first time since we'd arrived, and his expression wasn't particularly kind.

"Should I contact her? Are you implying that she's involved in some way?"

Way to turn the tables, like I was the snake in this equation. The guy had some nerve.

I smiled sweetly at him. "I understood that you were dating. Was I mistaken? Or do you not have the kind of relationship where you speak much?"

Oh, yes, I did. I'd just called him a man-whore, and I didn't even feel bad.

But he had a very different reaction than I'd expected. He leaned back in his chair, crossed an ankle over his knee, and smiled. He presented the ultimate picture of a man at ease. "Not that it's any of your business, but Gladys and I don't speak frequently over the phone. Neither of us is particular fond of idle chatter."

I wasn't sure who this guy was dating, but she didn't sound like Gladys. Gladys liked to chat. I glanced at Alex, but he looked as unruffled as Blaine.

Alex asked, "When did you last see Tabitha?"

"We've met frequently over the last few weeks." Blaine inclined his head. "To discuss various details of the selection ceremony."

That seemed...odd. And I needed the lowdown on this selection process. It kept popping up, and I was beginning to realize it wasn't a simple tick-the-ballot event. Not with Blaine's comments about oligarchies and my irrelevance.

Alex caught my eye and unobtrusively shook his head once. I could almost kiss him. Normally he kicked me in the shins when I was about to say something grossly inappropriate.

"And your last meeting with her?" Alex asked.

"I met with her last night." He paused, and I caught a

glimpse of unease. "I understand, Ms. Andrews, that you're close with Gladys?"

"I'm sorry, Mr. Waldrup, but what relevance does my relationship with Gladys have to this investigation?"

Frequent and late night meetings with a succubus, a woman who fed off men while having sex. Right. And there was the relevance. He was worried I would tattle on him to Gladys.

Blaine addressed Alex. In even, unemotional tones, he said, "Tabitha and I had a late evening appointment. I left her at the hotel sometime between eleven and midnight. You can confirm with the front desk attendant. I picked up a keycard on the way, and I believe left an impression on my way out." Then he turned with some deliberation to me. "There's no need for Gladys to find out about this. Don't you agree?"

I bit my lip. I wasn't about to promise this sleazebag anything.

"Did she have plans afterwards?" Alex asked.

He must have given up hope of me covering for his cheating rear, because he smirked and said, "I think that's highly unlikely. When I left her, she was falling asleep."

I was done with this guy. No way I was keeping his shady succubus dealings under wraps. What did Gladys see in him?

Alex wasn't looking too pleased with him either. He asked, "Do you know anyone who might've wanted to harm Tabitha? Besides you."

Go, Alex.

Blaine's smirk faded. "No. The most controversial part of her life was planning the selection."

"Whoa, really?" Both men turned to look at me. "Seriously? Neither of you thinks her sex life might have created some tension? Her very well-populated sex life?"

I bit the inside of my cheek. I'd forgotten for a split second that Blaine was primo bad-guy material. And I also sounded like I didn't approve of the poor dead woman's food source. I was a terrible person.

The men exchanged a look, then Blaine continued as if I'd never spoken—a sure sign of a big social gaffe. "Besides you, Alex, only Oscar and I have been named as candidates thus far, and neither of us would wish her harm. She's been very accommodating. In fact, it's rather inconvenient that we've been left without an organizer for the selection."

"As I'm sure you're aware," Alex said, "Cornelius is working on recruiting a replacement, but finding someone with the right connections on short notice poses certain challenges."

"Oh, I'm very aware, hence my concern. And also the reason I would most certainly not harm Tabitha." A look of annoyance passed across Blaine's face. "Are we done? I have other matters to attend to."

I touched my neck, and Alex—almost—rolled his eyes, but asked, "Did you feed last night?"

Blaine tensed. "None of your business."

"Let me be clearer. Did you feed on Tabitha last night?" Alex waited without expression for the answer.

I didn't think my poker face was half as good, because Blaine's gaze darted nervously to me.

"If I did, would it matter?" he asked.

That wasn't the response I'd have expected from a vamp who'd gorged on his prey until she'd been bled dry. Warning bells sounded in my head.

Alex didn't reply, just waited.

And waited.

Then Blaine cracked. Awkward silence for the win.

"It enhances sexual pleasure, as I'm sure you know. For both partners." He glanced between Alex and me, then frowned—probably because the stinker remembered my no-go policy on blood. "Maybe you don't know."

"I'm aware." Alex stood up. "Unless you have anything else to add? A confession, perhaps? No? I'll contact you with additional questions."

My heart skipped a beat when Alex asked the slimeball to confess. It looked like Alex was no fan of Blaine Waldrup's.

Blaine smiled, but it was pinched and mean. "Well then, I'll see you at the confirmation ceremony, if not before."

Alex headed to the door, and I hopped out of my seat like it was on fire then darted after him. As I practically ran through the house to the entryway—Alex could cover some serious ground without looking a bit rushed—a tiny woman watched me from a side room with wide eyes. She started to speak, looked behind me, and turned away. I was pretty sure it was the same woman who'd attempted to serve us when we'd arrived.

I glanced over my shoulder to find Blaine watching my retreat. I shivered, hopefully not visibly, and finished my undignified dash to the front door.

Alex held it open for me, and I scooted through.

I waited until both our car doors were shut, but not a second longer. "There was a lady, a little, tiny lady."

"The maid. I saw her. She looked like she wanted to say something."

"Good. Just checking I didn't imagine that. Human?"

"I think so." He frowned. "Maybe. I'm not sure."

Alex, not sure about someone's enhanced status? That was usually me.

"Before you ask," he said, "not a single spirit, elemental, or even a nasty demon inhabits the place. He must have found a way to protect the property." He pulled out of the parking lot and started down the drive at a good clip before he said, "You know I'm not actually considering the nomination."

I whipped my head around so fast, my neck hurt. Wasn't he? "I hadn't thought you were."

Had I? Actually, I hadn't thought anything, except—what the heck? I'd been so shocked that I hadn't considered the implications.

"I'm not."

Alex had mad skills: sword-wielding, speeding, air-bending—okay, I didn't know what manipulating air into a solid was called, but it was too cool to omit. "You seem more like a field operative to me."

"I agree."

I squinted at him. "So why are we talking about it?"

"You looked worried. But I won't actually accept the nomination. I'll show up to the ceremony on Friday and officially decline."

I wasn't worried. Scratch that. I *was* worried, but not about him being the next CEO. He'd be great at anything he did, and Alex had a deeply ingrained sense of justice and fair play that I would love to see in the next CEO of the Society.

No, my worries were more about losing him as a partner. Now that he'd planted the seed, I was definitely worried about that. Alex was an amazing partner. He was an amazing guy. He checked all the boxes for a bona fide hero: a strong moral code, a deep sense of personal responsibility both to the Society and me as his partner, amazing powers, excellent sword-wielding skills, a rumpled yet endearing appearance that some women might find incredibly hot—

"There's steam practically coming out of your ears." Alex looked at me. "What gives?"

"Ah, so tell me about this selection process."

"Did you read the orientation manual?"

Uh-oh. I might have lost the orientation manual. The one I wasn't supposed to remove from the Society's headquarters, and that I'd promised Alex I wouldn't lose. Oopsie.

"You lost it."

Must work on poker face.

"Give a girl a break. I was dealing with a murder at the time. I was a little distracted. And the beginning of orientation was all about the bathrooms." I stared out the window, watching as the countryside slid by at an alarming pace. "I don't pee. Where all that carrot juice goes, I don't know— but I definitely do not pee. It annoyed me that they were disbursing useless info."

"You know, not everyone shares that particular quirk."

"Wait." I peered at him. "You pee?"

Alex sighed. "So, about the selection."

9

(NO) DANCING NAKED IN THE MOONLIGHT

Ten minutes later, I was zoning out as Alex tried to explain to me the connection between Austin's founding families.

I clasped my hands together. "Oh, Lord, please make it stop."

"Hey, you asked."

And I had. But I hadn't expected a bunch of boring details. "But where are the blood sacrifices? The fancy clothes? The moonlit magic? Ooooh. The naked dancing in the moonlit forest." Not that I wanted to get naked and dance in the outdoors in Central Texas. Scorpions, fire ants, mosquitoes, wasps—need I say more? But I wouldn't mind watching Alex dance naked in the moonlight. Except it wasn't Alex I had a date with in a week. I might need to sort that out at some point.

"I hate to disappoint, but there's no evening wear or nudity. The selection is a daytime—clothed—event. It predates electricity, and since everything is easier in sunlight, it's held during the day. Imagine defending yourself against your feuding neighbors by candlelight."

I perked up. "Now, see, feuding neighbors—that's more like it."

Alex shook his head. "None of the seven families are feuding. That I know of. I was speaking historically."

"Gotcha. I guess that's good, since I don't actually want anyone killing their neighbors. In the abstract, it seems hillbilly-TV-drama exciting." Since I was about two seconds away from being laughed *at*—not with—I changed course. "Let me recap, CliffsNotes style. Once upon a time, there were seven founding families: assassin, thief, wizard, djinn, coyote, and some other ones."

"No, that's all. Originally, there were three coyote families, but two were ousted. And the djinn family is no longer closely connected to the U.S. but still holds on to a seat in the selection senate."

"Right. Like I said, I'm going for the cheap and dirty version. I'm sure you can remind me of the family connections should they prove relevant." I waited for his agreement, because family history might be important, and I really didn't want to try to remember all the so-and-so's fifth-cousin stuff.

"Got it. I'm in charge of Austin's political family tree." He tilted his head. "But you really should find that orientation manual."

Not taking the bait, I steered my thoughts firmly toward my quick and dirty summary. "Back to my story. Once upon a time seven families—all born enhanced, not made—converged in Austin in some way that I'm sure is very interesting but probably not relevant to this case. They created a governing body that eventually became the private corporation known today as the Society for the Study of Occult and

Paranormal Phenomena. The grand poohbah, or chief executive officer, is selected by the selection senate."

I paused to take a breath, and Alex said, "And the senate is made up of—"

"Hey, I was listening." Mostly. I was mostly listening. "The senate has fourteen members, seven born and seven made. Each founding family has one representative. Please tell me that's most of it. I feel like I've just taken a civics class."

"The CSO and current CEO can nominate candidates, as can members of the seven founding families."

Alarm bells rang in my head, and it had nothing to do with Alex's driving. "Wait a second. If Cornelius and *any* member of the seven families can nominate candidates, why are there only three of you?"

"Excellent question. And also one of the reasons Cornelius nominated me, I'm sure."

"You think something hinky is going on with the selection?"

Alex chuffed in amusement. "I hate to break it to you, but something hinky—as you put it—is always going on when leadership changes."

"Right." Except I didn't know what I was agreeing to. I was too distracted by the creeping sense of dread that was settling into my stomach.

We'd passed the gravel road and were back on a major highway again, and Alex was cruising at normal Alex speed, over the speed limit but not daringly so. Nothing remarkable was happening.

But if everything was unremarkably normal, why the dread?

Suddenly the knot in my stomach expanded, and I could barely draw breath.

"What's wrong?" Alex glanced at me. "Something's wrong."

"Pull over," I whispered. We were approaching a hill, a sizable one. It wasn't called the Texas Hill Country for nothing. "Now."

"There's a gas station just up the way a bit."

"Now!"

And Lord love him, he did. Or he tried to. He pumped the brakes and then stepped down hard on the pedal. As he shifted down to a lower gear, I realized the brakes weren't functioning. I clutched at my chest, now tight with panic. He'd been teasing me at the time, but Alex had once said a car crash could kill me now, new vamp powers and all.

Thank goodness Alex was a control freak about driving, because he seemed to know what to do. We *were* slowing down. No way I would have had a clue what to do if I were driving.

Of course, the hill didn't hurt our chances. Minus the fact we were getting distressingly close to the top of it. "Um, you see—"

"Yes. We're fine." After downshifting again, he pulled the emergency brake up slowly.

The car slid to a slow halt on the shoulder at the top of the hill. As soon as Alex put the car in park, I jumped out. It took Alex a little longer, because he had to wait for traffic to pass by. I was strongly tempted to shoot a few of those passersby the bird, given the fact they weren't changing lanes or slowing down.

"Hey, easy there. We're both in one piece. I think your car might even be okay—eventually." When I turned to glower at him, he said, "Your eyes are bleeding red."

"Oh. Sorry." I shaded my eyes, so anyone whipping by us

wouldn't see a strange glow. I waited a few seconds and then said, "Better?"

"No." He winced. "I hate to say it, but you actually look a little scary."

He cut off any reply by pulling his phone out and making a call.

I wanted to wallow in the awesome feeling of not being a fluffy bunny for once, but I was still too pissed about my failed brakes and the idiots zooming down the highway next to us.

With his phone tucked against his ear, he knelt down and looked under the car. "Star. Any chance you have time to do an autopsy on a car?"

When I looked at him like he'd lost his mind, he winked at me.

As I contemplated whether I was hallucinating or Alex had gone off the deep end, he chatted away with his go-to witch contact Star.

"Yes, I'm aware I only call when I have an emergency, and I know that makes me a terrible human being. I'll pay you lots of money." After a brief pause, Alex gave me a thumbs-up.

I laughed. Star and her four kids and their college funds —best motivation ever. At least some things were still predictable, unlike my beloved Grand Cherokee.

"How about that other thing? Is it done cooking?"

Uh-oh. That did not sound good. Star cooking something did not equal fresh chocolate chip cookies. Whatever was in the oven was apparently on schedule, because Alex looked pleased when he hung up.

He tapped away on his phone for a few seconds, then tucked his phone in his back pocket. "Anton's on the way to pick us up."

"Nooo." Even to my own ears I sounded whiny. In a normal tone, I said, "I could have asked Wembley."

"I thought you and Anton had some kind of non-aggression pact."

I made a grumbly noise. Technically, correct, but I really, really didn't like that guy. I'd been one wrong move away from getting offed by Anton during my transformation, and a girl didn't easily forgive or forget a near-death experience.

And speaking of near death... "What the heck just happened?" I wagged a finger at him. "I bet you're on board with Wembley's precog theory *now*. It's a heck of a lot easier to believe when it saves your life, isn't it?"

Alex leaned a hip against the Grand Cherokee. "We weren't anywhere near death. Trust me."

"Are you telling me my car wasn't sabotaged? Someone cut the brake line."

He crossed his arms. "Did they?"

I looked at him, the car, and then him. "Seriously?"

"Seriously. Cut the line, and there's no brake fluid. No brake fluid and a nice big warning light comes on—and your brakes don't work before you've even begun driving or maybe as you're just pulling out."

"Okay, then some crazy, murderous person put a hole in the line. You're splitting little itty-bitty hairs. Someone tried to kill us."

Alex tilted his head. "Technically, someone tried to kill *you*. And that was no hole. That was magic."

Suddenly the car autopsy comment made a lot more sense. If I'd been less angry, less rattled, then I'd have realized. Star was Alex's number one source for dissecting magic. He had his own set of wizardly skills, but Star had a completely different skill set.

Witches were made, not born, and the first step in the

process was to study magic. It seemed a bit backward to me, because how would you know about magic or what to study before you were a witch? But since study was the basis of witch magic, was it any surprise that witches had the niftiest, the most varied, the most marketable magic? Not that I'd say it out loud. Alex was a little snippy on the subject.

"Star is gonna give Kinky a thorough exam?"

"Kinky?" His lips twitched.

Alex had an eye for detail. He knew my car had a Kinky Friedman bumper sticker. "I'm serious. Am I going to be able to trust my car?"

Alex uncrossed his arms. "I'll make sure of it. I'll have her put some protection in place."

"Thank you." My eyes burned. "I love that car."

"Don't cry." Before I could start to think Alex was getting all sentimental on me, he handed me a hanky and said, "Anton will be here in a minute, and you get red streaks down your face."

I snatched the handkerchief and dabbed at my eyes. He wasn't wrong. And that was one bizarro un-vampish quirk most of the world hadn't yet discovered.

Once I'd dabbed at the corners of my eyes, I said, "What's cooking?"

"Ah." He looked a little uncomfortable, which made me even more curious.

"Is it to do with your other case, finding the amethysts?"

He closed his eyes and groaned.

"What? What did I say?"

"You might have just made a leap in logic that could be a very big clue."

"Hey, I'm the first to be super proud of myself, but I have no idea what you're talking about. Give me the scoop before mean Mr. Clean gets here."

"You know Anton hates that nickname, right?" He shook his head. "Of course you know that. What's cooking is a corpse dummy to replace Tabitha's corpse."

"The one currently located in the morgue—right. I was wondering how you were going to get a real autopsy done with Tabitha's body locked up. And wow, I just said that." I stopped, considered the facts, and decided on some clarification. "First, it is disturbing that Star can manufacture a corpse."

"But also pretty cool, right?"

The man knew me well. "Yeah, it really is. But what's even more problematic is that I think a 'real' autopsy is the magical kind. But we'll call it progress, or maybe indoctrination. What's the gem connection?"

He grinned at me. "I hadn't made one until now, but—thanks to you—I'm thinking an amethyst might be involved in Tabitha's death."

Anton's black Escalade pulled up, and Alex's face took on a much grimmer cast.

Mean Mr. Clean, known by those who didn't despise him as Anton, was a darker, grimmer, angrier version of the amiable and very likable Mr. Clean. He got out of his SUV toting some cables. "I'm towing the car to Star's place. Wembley is on his way to play taxi for you guys." Anton gave Alex a look and added, "Check your texts, man."

A short, stocky guy who looked like he might beat people up for a living got out of the passenger side of the Escalade. "Give him a break, Anton. The guy's eluded death for the hundredth or so time this year. It has to be exhausting." He caught my eye. "And distracting."

I waved cheerily. "Hey, enforcer guy."

With a charming, slightly gap-toothed grin, he lifted a hand in greeting. "Hey, new vamp lady."

I'd met Francis on an earlier case, and he'd been just as sweet then. I wished he had more seniority, so I'd see more of him and less of Anton.

"Get a move on, Francis." Anton was almost done hooking up the tow rope.

"Right, boss." Francis ambled up to me, moving neither faster nor slower than before. He held out his hand. "Keys?"

"You think he lets me drive?"

Softly and with a mischievous twinkle in his eyes, he said, "Oh, honey, I think he'd let you do whatever you like. You just have to ask."

Before I could deny it, Francis had left to retrieve the keys from Alex. This wasn't the first time someone had implied a romantic connection between Alex and I, but it was the most direct. Apparently, Alex was different around me. But how was I supposed to know that? I didn't get the chance to observe his behavior when I wasn't around, so I didn't have a baseline. And, quite honestly, even if it was true, the guy didn't have romantic feelings for me. He'd had more than ample opportunity to ask me out. He clearly knew how; the man dated *a lot*. And yet, he hadn't asked me out. Hadn't even hinted at it.

Alex lifted his hand, more salute than wave, as Anton pulled out. He came to stand next to me, but kept his gaze on the road. "Why are you blushing?"

"Am not." And I tried to think of not-embarrassing, not-hot things, because vamps didn't blush. It was getting old, hiding my oddities all the time.

"You're blushing. Our ride's here."

10

THE LOVE MACHINE

Nothing said former Berserker Viking, soldier of fortune, and badass vampire like a 1960s VW van in bright blue and white. It sparkled in the sun as it slid to a stop next to us.

"Nice," Alex said.

"Yeah, he just had the paint redone. Talk about someone who loves their ride."

Bradley's head poked out of the passenger window. "Shotgun."

I didn't have the heart to tell him that he didn't need to call shotgun when he was already in the front. Baby steps were a good plan with Bradley. He wasn't a very sociable sort of guy, and he hadn't had a lot of help with social situations until my elderly neighbor—pre-vamp transformation—had taken him under her wing. Since she'd been murdered, I was probably the closest thing to a mentor that he had. Hm. I would ponder the wisdom of that at a later date.

Alex opened the door, and I climbed in first. I wasn't sure how he'd managed it, but the interior of the van smelled amazing, like fresh-baked goods. Not even a whiff of patchouli incense intruded. Since Wembley hadn't eaten baked goods in a few centuries, I couldn't begin to guess how he managed to replicate the scent or why he'd want to.

"Where are we headed?" Wembley asked.

"Out to Star's, south of town." Alex stretched his legs out. He was a tall guy, so the fact that he could, meant the van was roomy. "I don't suppose you pick up Mallory's mom in this van when you guys go out."

Roomy backseats and my mother did not need to occur within kissing distance of each other. "And now I need to bleach my brain," I muttered.

"What was that?" Wembley met my eyes in the rearview mirror and grinned. "But no. When we go out, I take my in-town car."

"You have an in-town car? How do I live with you and not know that? Actually, never mind. If it involves my mother in any way, I don't want to know." I turned my attention to Bradley. "So, what brings you on this adventure? I'd have thought you'd be busy at your computer."

Bradley lifted up a laptop that had rested unseen in his lap.

"Why are you working in Wembley's van?" I asked.

"Repairmen in my apartment. Had to get out."

Uh-oh. My spidey senses were tingling in a very not nice way. "What happened to your apartment, Bradley?"

"Don't want to talk about it." He pulled his head up from his computer and looked over his shoulder. "Maybe tomorrow."

Wembley caught my eye in the rearview mirror again and shook his head.

"Hey, Wembley," Alex said, "what do you think of a succubus coming into contact with one of Bethia's amethyst stones?"

Wembley scratched his chin, and I winced as we swerved a foot to the right. "Could be interesting. You're thinking that's how the vamp managed to kill Tabitha? Sucking her blood wouldn't do it—not alone."

Alex's lips thinned. He wasn't a tolerant passenger even in the best of circumstances. "I figured the puncture marks were fake, since it would be almost impossible to subdue a succubus for long enough to remove a fatal quantity of blood. And that's assuming blood loss would kill a succubus."

"Ah, but with an energy-sucking stone, maybe Tabitha was weakened enough to be killed in a way that wouldn't normally be effective." Wembley looked intrigued by the prospect. I knew I was.

I found it increasingly easy to distance myself from the terrible acts happening around me. I hoped it was because I was becoming a better sleuth, learning to separate the harm done to the victims from the puzzle of finding the criminal. There was another possibility. Perhaps the wires that had crossed in my brain and rid me of certain anxieties during my transformation had only been the beginning. Maybe I was still changing. Maybe I was turning into the kind of vampire that just didn't care.

Wembley switched lanes in a jerky, haphazard fashion. A horn blared from behind us, yanking me back into the present, where a dead woman, missing jewels, and an attempt on my life were hollering for my attention.

"Wouldn't Tabitha be immune to a stone permeated with succubus magic?" I couldn't help thinking that if you had a cold, a cold virus didn't hurt you.

"Vampires can't drink vampire blood." Surprisingly, this statement came from Bradley. He sounded more like his old self. Maybe all he'd needed was a puzzle. Maybe he and I shared that.

"I'm not familiar enough with succubi to know the answer to that question," Alex said.

"Oh, I'm familiar enough with succubi," Wembley replied without an ounce of tact. "But those stones are an unknown factor. Of course, objects can take on magical properties. We've all carried witch-protection charms, but these are different. I've heard stories of magical items that have a history related to former owners, but who knows how much is tale and how much truth."

A bizarre thought occurred. "Is Bethia still alive?"

"No," Alex said. "I've been digging into her past since I started working on this case. She died publicly and her remains were burned."

I gave him a curious look. "How?"

With a wry twist of his lips, he said, "Stabbed in the heart by a spurned lover. A vampire, actually."

Wembley's bushy eyebrows—much tamer since he'd started chatting up my mother, but still full—lifted. "Anyone I know?"

"Knew. Victor Smythe was hanged for his crimes. Properly hanged with witch rope, not by humans, so he's definitely dead. Bethia had at least as many admirers as enemies, and the public nature of the crime meant that a lot of powerful paranormals were screaming for his execution."

"Any chance she was wearing the necklace when she was killed?"

"An excellent chance. The amethysts were her signature jewels," Alex said.

Given the fact Alex was investigating the whereabouts of the stones, it seemed certain he'd have checked out her inheritance. "I don't suppose you have any idea who inherited them."

"Oh, yes, a niece. But after the niece, I lost any trace of the necklace until stones started to pop up here in Austin. The niece disappeared into Russia, and I couldn't find further records of her."

I thought of the two good-sized stones that had landed in Austin. What were the chances someone took apart the necklace so many years ago and yet those two stones remained together or ended up together? "Wait, where did Bethia die?"

"New Orleans." Alex's eyes met mine. "You're thinking the stones never went to Russia."

"Yeah. A lot easier for them to make their way here from Louisiana than Russia."

"That was my conclusion, but I gave up on tracing the past into the present. There just wasn't enough information. I'm looking at the present and tracing back in time, or I was until Tabitha was killed." Alex leaned forward and said, "In case you guys missed it, I arrived on the scene after the police, hence our current excursion to retrieve a corpse dummy from Star."

"We're going to switch them out, Bradley," I said in a slightly louder voice. "Doesn't that sound fun?"

"No. I'll stay in the car." He never even lifted his head.

This was bad. Bradley loved sleuthing, and he didn't shy away from fieldwork. He aspired to ninja sleuth status, and that required pounding the pavement. Whatever had happened at his apartment—rat infestation, a broken pipe —it needed to get fixed fast. He didn't deal well with big, abrupt changes.

I leaned closer to Alex. "So, have you given much

thought as to how we're getting into the morgue to make the exchange?"

"We don't have to. There's been a clerical error in our favor. We made sure that the body was shipped directly to Star's funeral home. How did you think she was going to replicate it without having the original?"

I shrugged. Who knew with witches? But then a nasty thought intruded and I covered my face with my hands and I groaned.

"What? You think a clerical error is worse than breaking into the morgue?" Alex asked. He truly sounded confused. "Let me tell you, it's not."

I sighed. "That's not the issue." There went any hopes of my date with Gabe being on the up and up. I would totally have to lie about the Society's involvement. "There's a little thing called chain of custody. We've just busted it for the body. I really hope the murderer is enhanced, because if they're human, we probably just bombed any chance of them going to jail."

Alex shrugged. "I find it highly unlikely the perpetrator is human, given the punctures and the blood loss. Either it was a vamp or someone framing a vamp. Either way, the killer buys into at least the concept of vampires. But"—he met my gaze—"emergency response can handle it if we made a mistake."

"Not helping, Alex." I knew what "handle it" meant. Using code words for killing people didn't make it any more palatable. "I was human about two seconds ago." Bradley raised his hand, so I added, "And Bradley still is. You're talking about stepping outside the Society's justice system and into human vigilante justice. And Cornelius is actively trying to recruit Gabe as his inside source at APD. I know he already feels conflicted about his involvement with the Soci-

ety. If he found out that we were the cause of the mix-up...
Ugh. I bet he already suspects."

Who was I kidding? Gabe was clever. Of course he'd
suspect the Society's interference. Which put me in an
incredibly awkward position if he asked any questions.

Alex gave me an are-you-twelve look. "Enhanced and
human live in the same city. We share the same space.
There's occasional overlap."

He made it sound so simple, but it felt like...not murder,
but it felt wrong.

"Hey, kiddos, not to rain on your very moody parade, but
we're just about there," Wembley said. "You do realize we're
arriving during business hours. I can't imagine Star's
happy."

"Trust me, I know," Alex said. "I'm paying an inconvenience surcharge."

Which made me giggle. Star was a shark most of the
time. I would be with a passel of kids and education costs
rising.

"You're thinking about those six kids, aren't you?" Alex
shook his head. "You wouldn't be so amused if it was
your cash."

"Whatever—you're not broke. And it's four kids, not six."
I flashed him a cheeky grin. "Let's just hope all your cash
can get us some answers, like whether or not one of Bethia's
amethysts was involved."

As we pulled into the mortuary's drive, Bradley
announced into the silence, "I know who texted Gladys this
morning."

11

THE SCOOBY GANG

W embley slowed the van to a crawl. Smart man.

"How long have you known about the text?" I asked Bradley. "Never mind. Who sent it?"

"For fifteen minutes. You didn't stop talking until now. It came from Blaine Waldrup's personal cell."

Wembley chuckled and, when he finally got his mirth under control, said, "Well done, Bradley. Well done."

I poked a finger in Wembley's shoulder. "You shush. But he's right, Bradley. Really nice job. Next time you have an important piece of information, please interrupt me. Especially if I'm talking and talking and talking."

Bradley looked over his shoulder at me. "I don't think I'm supposed to do say you talk too much. Mrs. A wouldn't approve of that."

My cheeks hurt from trying not to smile. At least I could laugh at myself. I lacked the skill before I'd been transformed—so I had that going for me. "You don't have to say I'm talking too much. Just interrupt and let us know what you've found. You're an important member of the..." I looked at Alex and Wembley. What were we?

"Gang. Like on *Scooby-Doo*." Bradley nodded. A slight furrow appeared on his forehead. "Am I Velma?"

"I don't know, but Velma's cool, so if I were you I'd claim her." I couldn't believe we were stalled in front of a mortuary, two seconds from picking up a dummy corpse—made of who knew what—and we were discussing *Scooby-Doo*. Although I was not Daphne. I refused to be Daphne.

"We good?" Wembley asked.

"That depends. Bradley, you have anything else for us?" Alex waited patiently for Bradley to consider the question and formulate a response.

"I'm waiting for more information on the witness. I'll give you my full report when I have all of the information."

"Any first impressions?" Alex asked. "For example, do you think she's involved?"

"Weighing the available data, I would conclude that the probability is low she's either involved or enhanced."

Alex motioned forward when Wembley looked over his shoulder, and the van moved forward at a more reasonable clip.

Star was an odd duck. Once immersed in the witch life —whatever that meant—she now lived part-time as a wife and mother, part-time as a mortician, and part-time as a freelancing witch. I hadn't a clue how she balanced her life, but I knew she had a great deal of discretion in the types of jobs she took because she was the best of the best.

If I could choose any person in the enhanced community to be my gal pal, it would be Star. Wembley didn't qualify, but only because he was lusting after my mother, not because of his gender. Star had initially terrified me, then fascinated and terrified me, and now I was mostly fascinated and only a little terrified—primarily because she'd promised not to excise any of my memories unless I did something really, really bad or asked her to.

But it wasn't like Star would have time to gal-pal with me, so it was a moot point. I couldn't even imagine when she slept. Minus building fake dead bodies and other, similarly terrifying witchy activities, she mostly reminded me of a soccer mom. A soccer mom with some serious kick-butt powers. And contrary to Alex's objections, I was pretty sure that witches *did* get all the cool powers.

"I see that sparkle in your eyes," Alex said. "You're rhapsodizing over Star's witch gifts."

"Maybe." He really did know me too well.

"You can't afford her."

Wembley nodded in agreement. "You really can't. Maybe if you make it a century or two."

Bradley lifted his head from his computer. "Or invest wisely. You should invest your money."

I leaned over Bradley's shoulder as Wembley parked the van. "Do we need to have a chat about how I should be investing my money, Bradley?"

Unlike Alex and Wembley, Bradley hadn't accumulated his cash through sheer length of life. Bradley hadn't lived hundreds of years socking away cash, he was just good with numbers and charts and other things that made money make more money.

He shrugged and went back to typing on his computer.

I'd have to revisit investing when he was feeling more like himself. And also figure out what was up with his condo to have necessitated repairmen.

As soon as the wheels on the van stopped moving, Star, dressed in a light gray suit, exited the back door of the mortuary. Wembley obviously knew the drill, because he'd come around the backside of the building, where the bereaved wouldn't run into us.

Wembley, Alex, and I exited the van, but Bradley continued to type. Wembley motioned me to hurry up. "He's fine. I promised he could work while we ran all of our errands. Besides, he doesn't need to see this."

I paused at the open van door. "Be back in a bit. Just call my cell if you need anything."

Bradley nodded but didn't look up, so I pulled the door shut. I definitely needed to get the scoop from Wembley.

"Tick-tock, guys," Star called from the back door. As we got closer, she said, "I've got my assistant dealing with clients, and that's not her strong suit. So let's hustle."

I trotted to catch up with Alex and Wembley.

Star propped the door open with her tennis-shoe-clad foot, waving us through. As Wembley passed, she touched him on the shoulder. Odd, since the paranormal crowd tended not to be very touchy. Odder yet when she did the same thing to me. And then my suspicion trebled when I felt a warmth that was more than just body heat.

She followed behind me, closed the door, and then armed the alarm.

Wembley and Alex moved ahead into the next room, but I hovered near the door. "Did you just..." Except I didn't know what to ask. *Touch me with your hot hands?*

She grinned at me. "You're getting better, fluffy bunny. Yes, I did just feel you up—magically speaking." She moved toward the attached room, and I followed her. "Wembley, too, in case you're curious."

When I stepped into the adjoining room, I did a double take. Two women, identical in every respect, were laid out on two tables. Each had a sheet pulled high enough for modesty, but appeared otherwise unclad.

"It's disconcerting, isn't it?" Star said. "I made the copy, and I still find that seeing them so close together makes me uneasy."

"What's the copy made of?" I looked between the two women, trying to find some difference.

"Trade secret. But your medical examiner won't know the difference, that much I can promise you." She paused, "Well, he won't so long as he's human."

Now I really wanted to find the difference between the women, because obviously the copy had a tell. "Which one is the copy?"

Alex pointed to one of the women, and Star nodded.

Before I got sidetracked by the shiny magic, I asked, "And what you did to Wembley and me at the door, what was that about?"

"Ah. Well, your victim was bitten." Star moved to stand next to the real Tabitha. She pointed at the two punctures in Tabitha's neck. The pale pink of Star's nail polish looked incongruous next to the holes in Tabitha's flesh.

Wembley leaned down to examine the marks. "It looks like a vampire bite."

"It is. I'm certain of it." She moved away from the body to retrieve an apron. After she'd put it on and tied the stings neatly, she donned a pair of gloves. "I finished cooking the dummy, so I started on the autopsy. I didn't get far, but I did have time to analyze the wounds for trace amounts of vamp virus or saliva. I found both."

"I don't understand." The words escaped without a lot of thought, so when Star raised an eyebrow, I scrambled to think of why. It supported the theory that Blaine killed her —and I was just fine with that particular theory. Oops— Gladys. I was almost fine with that theory. "If a vamp did it, wouldn't he try to cover it up by removing obvious evidence like saliva? Especially a vamp with political aspirations?"

"You have a particular vamp in mind?" Star asked.

Without hesitating, Alex said, "Blaine Waldrup. He practically admitted biting her. And while I don't think Blaine is the cleverest of vamps, he's also not an idiot. I don't think he'd kill Tabitha and risk the chance of his confirmation falling through. The ceremony is days away. Plenty of time for an investigation."

"Whether he left evidence or not, bit her or not, let's not forget the obvious," Wembley said. "A succubus shouldn't die from blood loss."

"She would if she'd been simultaneously drained of energy." Star swiped a finger across the woman's face and showed us the lightened tip of her black nitrile gloves. "A little blood loss plus powder and you get the deceptive pallor. Even if she could be killed with a vamp bite, this one wouldn't have done it. So I poked around and found signs her energy levels were terminally low. See the wrinkling around the eyes, the softness around the jaw?" She tucked the sheet to the side and lifted Tabitha's right arm. "And this." Clasping the woman's arm, she pointed to an age spot on her hand.

Alex's eyes narrowed. "You think the energy and blood were removed simultaneously. That's a close variation on one of our theories."

Star pulled the sheet up over Tabitha and then clasped her hands together. "Do tell, preferably quickly. We don't want to be standing around chatting when the meat wagon comes for our dummy."

Alex cursed. "I was hoping for a little more time before they noticed the delivery mix-up. We'd hypothesized that one of the amethyst stones was involved, and that had weakened her enough to allow the killer's bite to do the rest."

Star looked intrigued. "A succubus's stone used on a succubus—maybe. If you can get me one of the two stones you've recovered, I can test the theory. Maybe tell you how the stone interacts with the body."

"Not a problem." Alex pulled a small black velvet jeweler's bag from his pocket. There were symbols stitched into the cloth. Familiar symbols.

I reached out, pulled by my curiosity, but Alex closed his hand around the bag. "Probably not a good idea."

"Those symbols trap the gem's magic inside the bag." Star retrieved a small tray.

Alex opened the bag and shook out the gem onto the tray. "The symbols are old magic. Better to stay away." And he tucked the bag back into his pocket.

Star sighed. "Alex." She sounded disappointed. To me she said, "Those symbols hold no power beyond their assigned function, which in this case is to shield anyone carrying the bag from the stone's effects. The symbols are nothing to fear. Some people are simply so stubborn that they can't shake old superstitions."

I knew I'd recognized them. The silvery symbols stitched on the bag were very similar, possibly the same, as the tattoos that Alex had over much of his torso. A shirt covered them completely, so I'd only seen them on the odd occasion when I'd caught Alex bare-chested.

Alex's lips thinned, and I thought he might not respond, but then he said, "You don't understand their power because you *wisely* chose to avoid the more arcane alchemic arts in your studies."

Star's eyes flashed. If my eyes bled red when I was angry, then Star's burned like a purplish-blue flame. It hurt to look her in the face. Her voice rose in volume and speed as she spoke. "You know *nothing* of my studies. You can hold on to old hurts and cling to your past and the mistakes you made, but don't blame the magic. Magic is nothing but a tool. You're the one who's turned it into a burden. You're the one who's convinced your only choice is to live like a martyr. Grow up, already, Alex."

I couldn't look away. It was like watching a car wreck, my parents fighting, and a fireworks display all at once. I forgot most of the time that Star and Alex had a history, but I didn't think I'd be making that mistake again.

She turned to me, her nostrils flaring and her eyes still bright. "You're this idiot's best chance at sorting himself out. Someday he's going to realize it, I just hope it isn't too late."

I had to squint and catch her in my peripheral vision to look at her. I wasn't sure exactly what she meant, but I did know that Alex was a very private person. She was acting more like his ex than his friend, and it wouldn't do their relationship any good. "Ah, maybe now's not the best time? You mentioned you were on a tight schedule, and your assistant...and, uh, and your eyes are pretty much blinding me."

Mentioning that my eyes were under attack made them water, which I always tried to avoid in public. So I closed them for a few seconds in hopes of staving off any blistering tears.

When I opened my eyes, I found Star standing in front of me, her eyes back to normal and a small smile tugging at her mouth. "I like you, Mallory."

I grinned, mostly in relief because I could see again. "That's cool, because I really like you. And we're good, right? Because I also find you terrifying."

"We're definitely good. By the way, that check I did on

you guys earlier was to verify that you didn't have succubus juice flowing through you." She glanced at Wembley and then back at me. "You guys are clear."

My first thought was, "Ewww," but then I realized how quickly the atmosphere had changed. Freakishly fast. It was as if the dramatic, glowing-eyed spat had never happened.

Then again, is it a spat when it's one-sided? Star had torn into Alex, and he'd just stood there. He hadn't looked mad, and his eyes hadn't popped with even a little spark. I wasn't sure why I found that noteworthy, because it was pretty typical Alex. He liked to be in control. It wasn't like I'd ever seen him lose his temper. Excluding when bad guys were trying to kill us. I was a strong believer that there should be a murderous-bad-guy-chasing-me exemption for all bad behavior.

Nuts. I was missing nifty witch magic in action. Star had started her experiment with the stone while I'd been pondering the mysterious depths of my partner's psyche.

And as I tuned back in to Star's witchy display of magic, that was when I saw the amethyst begin to glow.

12

SHINY, SPARKLY...A CLUE!

M agic glowed. Not always, but sometimes. I'd discovered that fact not long after my trans-formation.

But when it did, like the gorgeously sparkling amethyst Star held, then it was a beautiful sight. The stone glowed brighter as Star moved it along Tabitha's body. The stone glinted and sparkled so brightly that I wanted to reach out and touch it.

Alex clasped my hand. "You're like a kid in a candy store today."

I shrugged and gave him a sheepish look. I hadn't noticed I'd reached for the gem until he'd stopped me.

Star had wrapped a thin chain around the stone, so that it was cradled and could hang like a pendant. She held the chain, letting the stone swing freely several inches above Tabitha's body, and traced the length and breadth of Tabitha's body. Each time she neared the torso, the stone glowed brighter.

Star set the gem and chain on a small tray and then rolled a cart with instruments closer to the body. She flipped the sheet back, then, looking at me, she said, "You might not want to watch this."

As I was about to say, "No, I'll be fine," she sliced into Tabitha with a scalpel. I did a one-eighty and headed for the door. A short walk was looking good to me. "Be right back."

Since I wasn't sure what she was doing or how long it would take, a bathroom break seemed like a good choice. Just because a girl didn't need the facilities didn't mean she couldn't use the facilities.

It took a few false starts to find the bathroom. Once I did, I checked my eyes for signs of redness—not the glowing variety, the bloodshot kind. All clear. I'd escaped Star's heat gaze without any signs of tearing up. I washed my hands—because why not?—and then walked out of the bathroom, right into Alex.

He steadied me and then backed up. "Star found another stone."

"Whoa. I guess that answers the question about whether your amethyst case is related."

A thoughtful look crossed his face. "And possibly why Tabitha's body was removed and returned: a failed attempt to retrieve the stone."

As Alex and I entered the room, Star said, "Since the stone was in her stomach and not her intestines, I can guess that she'd swallowed it less than five hours before her death —but it's definitely a guess."

Wembley pulled up the sheet. "I don't see her eating an amethyst. Not for any reason, but especially not if she knew the effects this particular stone would have on her. You were at the hotel to interview her for the case, Alex, so what was her connection to the stones? And did she know what they could do?"

Star shooed us away. "Let me close her up."

Wembley, Alex, and I stepped away from the table, and Alex said, "So far as I know, she didn't have any knowledge of them. I'd made the appointment with her while I was still trying to follow Bethia's family tree to the present, and that's exactly what I told her: I had a few genealogy questions for her. Like djinn, succubi aren't that common in the States. I wanted to know if she might have a direct connection to Bethia or know who her descendants—more importantly, her heirs—might be."

Wembley nodded. "It's only recently, Mallory, within the last fifty years or so, that we've started to track on a broader scale the different identities that members of the enhanced communities assume. If you wanted to fade into anonymity, you could get lost with relative ease up until the last turn of the century. After that, it required a little work. But nowadays, it's much more difficult. There are institutions and organizations, like the Society, that track families and identity changes."

That sounded suspiciously like the source material for an app that Bradley had been commissioned to build. An app that had gotten him in some hot water with the Society not all that long ago.

"There must be individuals tracking us, too," I said. Wembley and Alex looked stumped by the change of direction. "You remember, there was that book Bradley told us about? The one that he used to make his app that calls Wembley Einarr, the Berserker, and has everyone rated by levels?"

"Of course. I could hardly forget," Wembley said. "I suppose there have always been the curious or the suspicious who collect information. I'm talking about more comprehensive databases put together by local enhanced governments. But about that app—"

"Hey, people," Star called out. "You're missing the good stuff."

All three of us turned as one and then crowded around the table. It looked like I wasn't the only one with a fear of missing out.

Tabitha was neatly stitched up, and Star had a small, goo-covered stone in the grips of a pair of forceps. I was a vamp; I could theoretically hold my breath forever, right? Because whatever was coating that gem reeked.

Holding the stone over a metal pan, she squirted it with a small bottle of clear fluid. I took a shallow breath and detected an antiseptic odor. Maybe alcohol.

Star removed her gloves and then picked up the stone with her bare hands.

"Should you do that?" I asked. Given the fact Alex had created a special bag to tote around its companion stone, her behavior seemed risky.

"Probably not, but it's much smaller than the other stone and doesn't have nearly the power." Star dropped it on a cloth-covered tray.

"But was it powerful enough to harm her?" Alex asked. "And what do you think of our theory? Well, your theory combined with our theory."

"If you're asking once consumed, if this stone in conjunction with a vampire bite is the cause of death, I'm eighty-five percent sure it was." Some of my disappointment must have shown, because Star added in a chiding tone, "I'm not done yet."

"Then it's Blaine." But even as I said it, I felt something was wrong. "The man fessed up to sleeping with her as late as last night. He practically admitted to biting her. He has to be our prime suspect."

"The timeline is a problem for Mr. Waldrup." Star smiled. "Time of death is midnight, give or take an hour."

Alex and I shared a glance. He looked about as convinced as me, yet there was the evidence. The timeline absolutely fit.

"What? What's that look?" Wembley asked.

Weighing the evidence against my gut wasn't fun, and I was particularly uncomfortable with the outcome this time. "Blaine told us himself that he was with Tabitha last night until eleven or twelve, but... I mean, don't get me wrong. I don't like him. He's oily, and self-important, and has some very disagreeable opinions about vampires and other enhanced groups."

Alex sighed. "But you don't think he'd be stupid enough to kill her and then fess up to both meeting and biting her during the time of death window."

"Or leave such obvious signs of feeding on her corpse. He didn't just bite her, he also failed to remove trace evidence. And he practically gloated over the great sex. He mentioned she was falling asleep when he left." A sick feeling made me stop and think about that. "You don't think she was..." I couldn't say it. Commingling death and sex in the same space in my head was making me feel icky.

"She might have been dying. Blaine strikes me as just self-absorbed enough not to notice." Alex pinched the bridge of his nose. "But anyone beyond the youngest of vampires knows how hard to bite, how long to drink to avoid causing damage or transforming a victim."

I felt the sudden urge to cover my mouth—more specifically, my undescended fangs. "Am I the only one who finds the idea of mixing biting—possibly death—with sex completely disturbing?"

"It's very unvamp-like of you," Star said. "Vamps usually

get that part of their brain melted away in the transformation." She tipped her head. It was almost impossible to see the angry-eyed woman from before in the heart-shaped face, sleek blond bob, and pink lip gloss. "I'd say most vamps are sociopaths, present company excluded."

"I belong to a group of psychos. Awesome."

"No, not psychos. Sociopaths. They're a completely different animal." She smiled at me. "But you've eluded that fate for now."

"For now." Like that was supposed to be comforting.

"Back to our case," Alex said, shooting me a sympathetic glance. "Since you're on a tight timeline, Star."

"Right." She clapped her hands together, and her no-nonsense demeanor slid back into place. "My question for you: how did this young lady consume the stone? It sounds like she had no knowledge of the Bethia necklace or the stones recent history in Austin."

Alex nodded.

"But whether she did or not, she wouldn't eat an amethyst." Star nudged the stone with the tip of her finger. "Even a small one would be noticeable in food. So who tricked her into consuming it? The man who bit her?"

Something sparked in my brain, but I wasn't sure what. Something to do with trickery. If I pushed, it wouldn't come to me any faster, so I moved on to another question. "Can you identify who bit her, from the saliva? I might have my reservations about Blaine, but the evidence is pointing to him and we have to build a case."

"No luck there. I mean, maybe if I had a larger sample size. Then I could experiment with some different options... try a few... Hm." She spun around to face Wembley. "How about you donate some spit?"

Wembley scratched his jaw. "As disgusting as that sounds, I suppose I could make the sacrifice."

"It'll give me something to experiment on until I get the process right. But it could take a few days."

A few days in a magical murder investigation was a long time. We had to have a faster way to test the saliva.

And we did. If only all my brain cells were firing, I'd have thought of it sooner. I was a grade-A idiot, since the best option available to us also liked to drool on my pillow every night.

"Can't Boone match the saliva to the donor?"

Star turned a critical eye on me. "The djinn's hound. That might work." She pulled on another pair of gloves. "Maybe."

After searching through a few drawers, she returned with two small glass sample jars, a quart-sized Ziploc freezer bag, and gauze. She tore open the sterile gauze pads and swiped Tabitha's wound. She nodded at me. "Open those."

I unscrewed the sample jars, and she placed a gauze pad in each. I held out the baggie last.

"Nope. That one's for me. I don't know exactly how your hound works, but since he hasn't met me, I'm giving you a sample of me." She pulled out a hair from her head, grabbed a gauze pad and wiped it across the pulse point at her neck, and then chucked both in the Ziploc. She narrowed her eyes and gave me the Wicked Witch of the West glare. "Burn it when you're done."

Wide-eyed, I nodded. "I'll burn it. Not the plastic?"

"All of it."

"Right. Sure thing." I bit my lip. "And thank you." I tucked the folded plastic bag in my front pocket, then tucked the glass sample jars into my purse.

Wembley looked relieved, probably because he got to keep his spit.

Alex looked at the dead woman and shook his head. "Blaine just doesn't feel right." He pointed a finger at Wembley. "Don't start with the precognition theories. Investigator's intuition is not precognition. The bare facts might fit, but we're missing something."

The door leading to the front of the mortuary flew open with a thud, and my heart lodged itself in my throat. I caught a blur of movement in my peripheral vision just a hair later.

Gabe walked in followed by a tall, middle-aged, and apparently human woman. She had to be the assistant, since she was also dressed in a gray suit, though several shades darker than Star's, and carried a tablet.

"I tried to explain that you were with clients, Mrs. Kowalski." The woman looked appalled that she'd failed in her duty to protect her employer and clients from an unseemly intrusion.

Not that we were regular clients, which made me wonder if other sorts of odd happenings took place at Kowalski Funeral Home of Buda.

"Color me surprised," Gabe said, looking anything but. "If it isn't the amateur detective squad, making my life more difficult by the moment."

His words weren't particularly harsh, but he looked pissed. Seriously pissed.

Uh-oh. Maybe I didn't have to worry about what I was wearing on that date after all.

13

AND THEN THE LIES BEGIN

Gabe's face was tense, and he zeroed in immediately on Alex. "Maybe you'd like to explain what you're doing with my victim's body?" He gestured to the dummy Tabitha.

Oh, no. The two Tabithas. How were we going to explain that? Gabe knew about the Society, but he'd only dipped a toe. This was five levels beyond toe-dipping. I shot a panicked look in the direction of the real body—the one Gabe hadn't yet noticed—and saw a covered corpse. I exhaled.

Gabe glanced in my direction but didn't get a chance to speak, because Star approached him, stepping neatly between him and the real Tabitha's corpse.

She extended her hand. "Stephanie Kowalski, the owner of Kowalski Funeral Home. And you are?"

I blinked. Stephanie? Although...the blond hair, the petite frame, the pixie face. I supposed that fit. The name Star conjured tats, black lipstick, and heavy eyeliner in my mind's eye. Or it had before I'd met the real Star. But Stephanie did suit her soccer mom persona.

"Detective Gabe Ruiz." And that was all he said. My guess was that he suddenly realized it was possible not everyone in the room was in on the paranormals-in-Austin secret.

Star addressed her assistant. "I'll be glad to help Detective Ruiz clear up this error, Mrs. Parish. Thank you."

The poor, flustered woman fled. A detective showing up and demanding entry could hardly be expected as normal fare for a funeral home, but I'd think someone working with the bereaved would have a little more equilibrium in times of crisis. I could see why Star wasn't thrilled to let Mrs. Parish deal with the clients regularly.

"Now," Star said, "as for this error, we stopped processing the body as soon as we discovered the problem." She waved at the corpse dummy. "We left her exactly as she was, didn't even place her back in a body bag. We await your instruction."

A muscle twitched in Gabe's jaw. It had to be killing him not knowing whether Star was one of us. Clearly he suspected, but had his special sort of ability given him a clue? He'd said it didn't work all the time. Finally, he said, "The coroner has an assistant on the way. He'll supervise the removal of her body."

Star nodded. "Then we'll plan to make further arrangements for Ms. Waters when she's returned to us."

Gabe's eyes narrowed. "I'm sorry, but the family hasn't been notified yet. I'm not certain who will be handing the arrangements for them, but that will be their decision once the body is released."

Star didn't pause. Without skipping a beat, she said, "All of the local enhanced corpses are handled by Kowalski Funeral Home."

Gabe blew out a breath. "I knew it."

"But not entirely," Star murmured. She managed to be polite and not antagonize him, while still completely controlling the conversation. It was unnerving.

Gabe turned to me and said, "Couldn't have given me a hint, could you?"

Alex saved me from responding. "No, actually. Whether to expose her identity to a human—one who's also a cop—is Stephanie's sole prerogative. It's bad manners to out one's friends, acquaintances, and business associates."

I shrugged. "I'm new, so I defer." The less I said, the better. And I did my darnedest not to look at the pink elephant in the room. That was proving difficult. Telling myself not to look wasn't really helpful, so I alternated between that and telling myself what *to* look at. *Don't look at the real dead body. Only look at the fake dead body. Not the real one, only the fake one.*

"Are you all right?" Gabe asked. "You look a bit funny."

I shook my head slowly and tried to clear my face of any telltale signs of stress. "Fine." Then I remembered the circumstances of Tabitha's death and frowned. "I mean, it's upsetting, what happened to that woman."

Gabe laughed. "Don't tell me you guys aren't on the case. Why would you be here, otherwise?"

"We didn't touch the body," Alex said. He was oriented to the corpse dummy, and the implication was that *this corpse*, the one in front of him, hadn't been touched.

In fact, all of us had oriented our bodies to face the corpse dummy, as if by pretending the real corpse wasn't in the room, we could make it disappear. Too bad Star didn't have some sneaky way to make that body disappear...or did she? I was tempted to look and see if it was still there. The back of my neck itched with the urge.

"You guys aren't going to tell me what's going on, are you?"

I just gave him a wide-eyed, innocent look, because it was the best I could manage. But Alex said, "Not a chance," and Star said, "No."

Gabe closed his eyes for a second then sighed. "You guys manufactured the glitch so that you could get a look at her. I get that you want to see if there's a paranormal connection, but you can't interfere like this. Not when there's an active investigation, and not when what you're doing could tank any chance of us finding and then prosecuting the offender. An offender who might be human."

"Not a human." I winced after the words had escaped. Man, was I bad at this whole keeping-secrets thing. Yet another reason to put off seeing my mother. I could just imagine it. Hi, Mother. No, not a diet. I'm a vampire, and I might turn into a psycho any day now, so be sure to lock your doors at night.

Gabe leveled me with an intent stare. "What did you find?"

Alex took a step closer to me. "Do you think that's a good idea, *Detective* Ruiz?"

The not-so-subtle reminder of Gabe's precarious situation—trapped between being the good, honest cop he was and keeping the secret he knew was in everyone's best interest to be kept—was a little low, but probably necessary.

While I'd been watching that conflict play out on Gabe's face, Alex had inched closer. He put a hand on my back, gently, but still a reminder that I needed to keep silent.

Mrs. Parish appeared with a young man who had to be the coroner's assistant.

As she ushered him into the room, Gabe assumed a neutral, inscrutable expression. "So if I have any more questions, I'll be in touch." He pulled his wallet out and extracted a single business card, which he handed to Star. Meeting her gaze, he added, "And if you have any information for me, give me a call. My cell number is at the bottom."

Star accepted the card, nodded briskly, and then moved toward the door.

Wembley pointed to the back door. "If you'll let me out, I'll just go check on Bradley."

Bradley—I'd forgotten all about him working diligently in the car. Hopefully he hadn't been ambushed by Gabe. And clever of Wembley to make sure the coroner's assistant didn't accidentally stumble on him and try to strike up a conversation. Bradley could usually keep his mouth shut, probably better than me, but he seemed to be in a strange place right now.

Star punched in the code to open the door, and after Gabe had left, she told the assistant to pull around back where he could get closest to the door.

After the assistant had disappeared through the back door, Alex said, "And here I was thinking that your impulse-control issues were so improved."

"Ugh, I know. I'm sorry. Maybe that date on Friday isn't such a good idea."

Alex raised an eyebrow. "No comment."

"You haven't changed, Alex," Star said from across the room. "Still can't see what's right under your nose."

I spun around to look at her. "Does every enhanced being running around in Austin have fabulous hearing?"

"Many, but mine's not even switched on right now. You're just not that quiet." Star turned to Alex with an expectant look.

He met her gaze evenly. "I see just fine, Star."

The assistant returned, and it seemed like a great time to

skedaddle. I might still have some hurdles on the impulse-control front, but I was becoming a master of avoidance.

On another avoidance front, I decided it was probably best to forget Star's tirade over alchemic symbols, Alex's stupidity, and me being his last hope. Who knew what that meant? And I didn't think Star or Alex would be eager to rehash the conversation. Star, because she was back to her brisk, no-nonsense self, and Alex, because he was Alex.

Star hustled us out the back door, and as we exited, said, "Don't call me; I'll call you. And not until after we're closed." Then she firmly shut the mortuary door behind us.

I squinted up at Alex. "Was she talking about my Grand Cherokee or the rest of the autopsy?"

He switched to stand on my left, so I wasn't staring up into the sun. "Probably both. Your Jeep's in the funeral home's garage, by the way. Anton texted me earlier."

We were passing the coroner's van, halfway to the Vanagon, when Alex stopped. He looked at me, even opened his mouth, but then he took a breath and just kept walking.

If I didn't know better, I'd say he'd considered—ever so briefly—explaining Star's tirade. But I did know better, and Alex wasn't about to share his personal life with me.

14

WHODUNIT?

Wembley was tooling down the freeway, headed back to Austin, when Bradley broke the silence. "So who did it?"

No one jumped to answer, and I was pretty sure I knew why. "Let's get a head count. Who thinks the evidence points to Blaine?"

Wembley kept his right hand on the steering wheel and raised his left. Alex and I both raised our hands. Bradley kept on typing.

I wrinkled my nose. "And who thinks Blaine did it?"

Bradley stopped typing and raised his hand. He was the only one.

I groaned. "You're probably right, Bradley. It just *feels* wrong."

"If the clues lead to Blaine, Blaine did it." Bradley paused. "Or the clues are false. Or we didn't interpret the clues correctly."

"So we need to disprove the clues or reinterpret them," I said. "You're right, Bradley. Sometimes it's helpful to boil everything down and make it simpler."

Bradley looked over his shoulder at me. "Simpler is changing your vote, and you're welcome."

Since I didn't want to change my vote, or rather my gut didn't want me to, I considered which clues we might disprove or could be false. "As an exercise only, let's exclude the vampire angle."

"The one solid lead we have?" Wembley grumbled. "No, no. I get it. It doesn't quite add up." Then he grinned at me in the rearview mirror. "And I have great faith in your intuitive precognitive abilities."

I laughed. It was getting to the point of ridiculous, how firmly he was convinced, even in the absence of proof... I stopped laughing as I remembered our magicked car ride earlier.

Alex cringed. "Don't. Just don't. He doesn't need any encouragement."

I nodded. Probably best to keep those angsty precog feelings of impending doom to myself. "Like Bradley said, let's look at the evidence. Do we trust our clues?"

Bradley raised his hand. He did that occasionally, though we'd been weaning him off it. "We don't know who sent the text to Gladys. I gave you the owner of the phone, Blaine Waldrup. The owner isn't always the person who uses the phone. Also, I was unable to retrieve the text message. We don't know what the message said."

"That's true," I said. "We only know that Gladys had knowledge of Tabitha's death. I didn't think to ask her how she knew."

"I wouldn't trust what she tells you, not with all the time she's been spending with her glamoured-to-the-gills boyfriend," Alex said.

I whipped my head around to look at him. "What? What do you mean glamoured?"

Alex didn't say anything.

"You forgot our little gal sees past most minor glamours without realizing it." Wembley looked at Alex in the rearview mirror, and it was hard for me to read the expression on his face. "Maybe there's an overdue conversation you should have with her."

Alex didn't seem to appreciate the nudge. "What Wembley is referring to is a genetic hiccup that I inherited from my mother's side of the family. I have a very minor glamour that I can't shake." He shot Wembley a look that predicted serious payback. "Not that I haven't tried to remove it. Blain has one as well, but his is intentional."

"And I don't see them," I said. "I don't get it."

"Some people are immune." Wembley waggled his bushy eyebrows at me. "And you hit that jackpot."

"Uh-huh. And how do you know that?" I was trying to choose my words carefully. Mostly because Bradley was in the car, and I suspected I was about to be properly pissed off.

Alex shot me an apologetic look.

Wembley looked entertained by the whole thing. "What did you see when you looked at Blaine?"

I didn't think twice. "Oily used car salesman."

Alex chuckled. "Spot on."

"Okay," Wembley said, "but give me some specific physical attributes."

"Medium height, dark blond hair, bland features." I tipped my head, thinking back to his interview earlier that morning. "Posh clothes, beautifully cut but not expensive enough to hide the beginnings of a beer gut. Oh, gross. I guess that's a blood gut." My scalp crawled. I shook off the creepy-crawly feeling and tried to recall some other detail. "Maybe brown eyes? Or hazel? I don't remember."

Wembley snorted in amusement and the van swerved. "I'm not immune, and I'd say tall, light blond hair, tan, trim, and athletic."

My mouth opened as he listed attributes I wouldn't attach to the sleazy guy I'd met. "Uh—no."

"And what about Alex?" Wembley asked. He really wasn't worried about retribution. I know if I was him, I wouldn't be looking forward to my next training session with Alex.

It was just about impossible for me to imagine Alex, a man very uncomfortable with illusion and especially it's stronger cousin persuasion, walking around with some kind of glamour stuck to him. I gave him a speculative look, and decided I'd be brutally honest.

"Six one??" I looked at him for confirmation.

"A little over six two."

"Okay, either way, tall. Not particularly big, but broad shoulders. Dark hair with a touch of gray and always a few weeks overdue for a haircut, rarely clean-shaven but more than a five-o'clock shadow. Frequently rumpled." I pursed my lips, examining him. "Blue eyes and lots of lines, likes he's been out in the sun and refuses to wear sunglasses."

He didn't look thrilled to be the center of this kind of attention, but, honestly, he was hot and confident, so I wasn't sure why.

Wembley startled me out of my musings with his next question. "Ever seen him naked?"

I pointed at Bradley and made a face at Wembley.

Talking about nudity and anything remotely like sex in front of Bradley was like taking your kid brother to a movie with sex scenes. Ick.

Alex coughed. "He means without a shirt. Right, Wembley?"

Oh. Ooooh. I looked at Alex, and he nodded.

"Yes, and he's covered in tattoos." I omitted the fact that I'd been tempted to inspect them up close and personal. I didn't mention it, because I'm a hulking big coward.

Wembley snapped his fingers. "See. Most people can't see those. Not unless you already know they're there."

"Wait, do different people see you in different ways?"

Wembley pointed at me. "A prize to the little lady with baby fangs."

A few pieces fell into place. "That's where the weird 'clean-cut sheriff' comment came from."

Alex looked at me like I was nuts.

I wagged a finger at him. "No, no. I am not the crazy person here. My designer said you looked like one of those sheriffs in an old western—clean-cut, strong, and silent. And I thought she was crazy, because you're always a little rumpled." I gave him a stern look. "Hang up your T-shirts when you pull them out of the dryer. Or fold them. One or the other." I lifted my hands in exasperation. Over his shirts. His glamour. Whichever.

"I can't help it." Alex gave me a disapproving look. "Not the shirts, the glamour. Except for the tattoos. I push the glamour to hide them when I can."

It was like he could read my mind. And why was I obsessing over wrinkled T-shirts? I didn't feel any of my previous OCD traits resurfacing. No, it was just easier to displace than deal with the fact I'd been bamboozled by someone I considered a friend.

He looked sorry.

I sighed. Maybe not bamboozled. But he'd perpetuated a monster-sized lie of omission.

"Are we going to solve the case? We're getting close to my exit." Bradley didn't even look up from his computer.

"You're absolutely right, Bradley," I said. "We need to focus on the case. Why don't you come home with us, so we can finish discussing the clues? And if you want to work for a little while, we can set you up in the study. You're not still working on the case file, are you?"

"No. I'm trying to find the person who broke into my apartment."

I did a quick rewind to make sure I'd understood. Nope, couldn't be right. "I'm sorry, what was that?"

"The break-in at my apartment," he repeated, "I'm trying to find the perpetrator."

Wembley winced at the nasty look I shot him. How could he not find some way to tell me that? Poor Bradley. The guy had to be devastated.

"One more secret today and my head might explode," I mumbled. I knew Wembley and Alex would hear. Louder, I said, "Bradley, I am so sorry that happened to you."

"That's okay. I think I found him. I'm posting a bounty now. I should have it all taken care of by tonight."

Maybe I was unwell and hearing things. Maybe someone had slipped me a massive, hallucinogenic—for vampires—dose of caffeine. Or maybe the world was about to end, and I'd just missed the signs. "Wembley! Pull the van over *now*."

15

BOUNTIES, BAD GUYS, AND BINGO

W embley exited the freeway immediately. It turned
out to be the exit for our house, anyway, but then
he pulled into the first gas station we came upon. "I'll just
fill up while you sort out...this."

Some former Berserker Viking he was.

Granted, I'd have jumped out of the van myself if I
could, but I couldn't abandon Bradley to the mafia or the
cops. If hiring a contract killer didn't put you in the sights of
one or the other, then all of those based-on-a-true-story,
made-for-TV movies were a big, fat pack of lies.

This was Bradley, so a carefully considered strategy—
with close attention to detail—had the highest probability
of success. And if I had more time, I'd have tried, but he kept
typing, so I leapt on the first reasonable argument that
popped in my head. "Bradley, you know that hiring
someone to kill another person is illegal."

Bradley was all about the rules, and laws were just a
bunch of rules.

Alex looked like he was about to explode with laughter,
and that made me want to murder him. Counterproductive,

since I was trying to prevent a murder. Just to make myself feel better, I punched him in the arm. Unfortunately, that just made it worse.

He muttered, "Bathroom," then hopped out of the car quicker than a flash. I eyeballed him a few feet from the van, chuckling to himself.

Bradley stopped typing. "I said bounty, not hit. A bounty is a reward for a specific task. A hit is when you hire someone to kill another person."

Relief flooded through me, right up until I realized he might have played around with the words to justify his less-than-legal plans. "What is the bounty for, exactly?"

"The name of this man." He lifted up his laptop to show me a high-quality profile shot of a stranger standing in his study. The picture looked like a screen capture from security footage.

I could have wept in relief. "You have a security camera."

"Of course."

Then another troubling thought occurred. "What are you going to do with his name once you have it?"

"Talk to Cornelius. I promised to let him know who it is, and then he said we could discuss options."

I exhaled in relief. "You've been in touch with Cornelius." I really didn't give Bradley enough credit.

"At four-oh-five yesterday when I came home and discovered the break-in. I promised when I signed the confidentiality contract with the Society to report any future suspicious activity connected to the gaming project app." He frowned. "The contract didn't define 'suspicious.' I had to infer."

Now my head really did hurt. That stupid app. It just had to keep coming back and causing trouble.

"Someone breaking in to your condo counts as suspicious. What made you think it was related to the app?"

"The intruder didn't appear on the security footage from the garage."

"Oh, gotcha." I'd learned a few weeks ago that vamps could mask themselves from electronic recording devices, but I hadn't gotten around to figuring out *how* they—we— did it yet. "He masked himself from the garage footage, but he didn't know you had a security camera, so he didn't know to mask himself from it."

Bradley nodded. "My neck is starting to hurt. Do you have any more questions?"

I leaned over the edge of the front seat, so he didn't have to twist around to speak to me. "Why couldn't you find this guy yourself? You're like Superman on the Internet."

He almost smiled. "I had your case. But mostly because my client moved up the deadline for a project." Bradley blinked at me. "I'm charging him lots of money to do it early."

I bit my lip to keep from laughing. "It's cheaper to pay the bounty."

"Yes. I'm expensive."

Then I did grin. "I bet you are."

He looked longingly at his computer.

"Get back to it. I'll fetch the guys. They have to be done filling up by now."

Bradley didn't look up. "They finished three minutes ago."

Lesson learned. Bradley was not only more of a sleuthing ninja than me, he was also a rock star among his own kind. Then again, I'd known that. He really was like Superman on the Internet.

I opened the door and waved at the gossiping men of

action. When they didn't hotfoot it back to the van, I got out and joined them. "It's safe, promise."

"You're not gonna make me pull off the road again?" Wembley asked.

"Knock it off. How was I supposed to know he was just outsourcing a little bit of face-recognition work?"

"I figured it was something like that. Bradley's a good kid." Alex didn't even blink to call a thirty-something-year-old man a kid. But when you were as old as dirt...

"How old are you, exactly?" I asked, trailing behind him to the van.

"Emotionally or physically?"

Since I got a nice rear view as he climbed into the van, I almost made a cheeky remark about aging and appearance. And he deserved a little razzing after keeping me in the dark all this time about his glamour problem. I was thankfully saved from an embarrassing remark by the bell, or a bell. Bradley's computer, which had been completely silent throughout the trip, dinged twice.

"Bingo," Bradley said.

That was a decidedly un-Bradley-like word, so I couldn't help asking, "You finished your project?

"No. I'm meeting my source at bingo this evening. At the senior center."

"I'm assuming this is some shady hacking-type source?" When Bradley reluctantly nodded—probably because my adjectives weren't as concise or precise as he'd like—I said, "Looks like we're all going to the senior center tonight, boys."

Wembley and Alex groaned.

Bradley frowned at me. "You can't all come. It doesn't work like that."

I raised my eyebrows. "You think we'll chase off your

shady information dealer? Why does he have to see you in person, anyway? Can't you just pay in bitcoin or PayPal or something?"

Wembley guffawed.

That probably wasn't good. When the oldest guy in the van thought your understanding of marginally legal to illegal computer transactions was laughable, you might be in trouble.

"I've worked with this source before. She doesn't take bitcoin." Bradley sighed. "Or PayPal."

"Cash?" I hoped it was cash. My mind skittered to other unsavory things, but I really didn't see Bradley trading sex for info. "Wait, is your source an employee or a client of the senior center?"

"A resident. This retirement community has its own senior center. Can we talk about this later? I need to finish more work on my project if I'm going to have time to shop, meet Dot, and complete my project on time."

"Yes, Bradley," Alex said. "And don't worry, we'll just drive you and wait in the car. Close if you need us, but out of the way."

I opened my mouth to protest, but stopped myself. Not two seconds ago I was telling myself that I underestimated Bradley. Time to give the guy a little credit and a little space. Besides, if I was in the car, I could still sneak in as a bingo player after he'd gone inside.

"And we're home." Wembley sounded relieved. "I bought you an extra whiteboard for the study, so you'll stop stealing that one I put by the front door. We can use it to finish out our clue and suspect analysis."

"Thanks, Wembley." I'd have hugged him, but he was busy parking. Minus his interest in my mother, he really was the best roommate ever. "If we do it in the kitchen, Bradley can get a little peace in the study."

Bradley gave me a thumbs-up as Wembley put the van in park.

"Let's meet in the kitchen in five. That gives me time to give Boone a break." No one complained, so I figured that would work.

By the time I hit the door, I had a weird feeling, and by the time I'd punched in my lock code, Alex must have too, because he stepped between me and the front door.

He motioned us to move back, pulled out his sword from thin air—which still boggled my mind—and stepped inside.

I'd forgotten my own sword in the back of the Jeep, which was now stashed at Star's. Big oops. In a stage whisper, I called out, "Tangwystl."

But nothing happened.

"Tangwystl," I called, a little louder. Still nothing. My oops was looking more like an epic fail. Tangwystl must be miffed that I'd forgotten her in the car. I turned to find Wembley headed for the garage. I lifted my hands in the universal what-the-shoot-man-heck-are-you-doing gesture.

He didn't reply. We needed to work on our silent communication.

Alex had been inside and awfully quiet for way too long.

I tried my tetchy living sword one more time. "Tangwystl!"

Alex appeared in the front door still in possession of all of his limbs and not leaking any vital fluids. "Quit calling for your sword and get in here."

I drooped in relief.

"That's what you get for leaving your sword lying around." He swung the door wide and waved Bradley and me inside.

Feeling adequately shamed for my forgetfulness, I shuffled inside...to find Cornelius in my living room. "What... Ah, why—"

"I do occasionally leave the office and get out in the field, Ms. Andrews."

Uh-oh. I wasn't just in trouble with my sword. Cornelius only called me Ms. Andrews when he was displeased. Seriously displeased. "Oh, no. What did I do this time?"

His piercing eyes drilled into me, and I called one last time, very quietly, "Tangwystl?"

16

WHODUNIT? FOR REALS

For a man who was barely of average height and not particularly broad, Cornelius Lemann managed to be intimidating as heck. His neatly trimmed gray beard didn't soften his features like it did some men. He was all edges and piercing eyes.

Wembley broke the tension when he said, "Tsk, tsk, Mallory. Haven't I taught you better? Never cede unearned ground. The question is not what you've done, but why the CEO of the Society has broken into your home."

He'd slipped in through the interior door in the garage, and he was packing—a sword, not a gun. He'd recently slipped back into a regular training routine and had given up guns. He and Alex swore a magic sword wielded by a trained swordsman trumped a gun every time. I was reserving judgment.

"It hasn't been the best day," I said. "How about we just call this a learning experience? So why *are* you here?"

Bradley raised his hand.

Cornelius seemed unsurprised by Bradley's off-kilter behavior. "No, Bradley, this is not related to the unfortunate incident at your condo. I'm confident that you'll pass along any pertinent information as it becomes available. And, once again, our thanks for beginning the preliminary investigation in this time of strained resources."

My blood pressure ticked up a notch. Anyone but Bradley should be investigating the break-in, and Cornelius should never have taken advantage of him.

"Your eyes, Ms. Andrews." Cornelius didn't blink. Given his unruffled demeanor, my glowing red eyes weren't as scary as the silver laser beam eyes he could turn on at will. "Bradley approached me, and he assured me that working on the case would allow him to regain some sense of control. Do you find it's helped to investigate?" Cornelius directed the question at Bradley.

"Yes."

And I'd agree. Even in the few hours I've been with him today, I'd seen an improvement.

Alex had stood quietly to the side, swordless, during this exchange, but he finally spoke. "Let's cut to the chase. You're not here just to check in, especially without visible means of transportation. What's with the covert visit?"

"I decided a low-key, under-the-radar chat might be best." Cornelius leveled Wembley with a steely stare. "Not for any nefarious reason, simply as a precautionary measure. It seemed wise, given the people being investigated and the information I'm bringing you."

Wembley and Cornelius had a history that was murky but obviously contentious. Someday I'd get the full story.

Wembley placed his sword on an end table. Looked like a pointy hazard waiting to slice someone open to me, but better than him waving it around in Cornelius's face.

Cornelius inclined his head then gestured at the sofa. "May

I?" Once we were all seated—except Wembley, who hovered on the edge of the kitchen and the living room—Cornelius asked, "What have you discovered so far about Tabitha's murder?"

Alex brought him up to date: the discovery of the stone, the confirmed vamp bite, the likely cause of death being the combination of the ingested stone and the bite, Blaine's amorous activities with Tabitha and the timeline of their last meeting, and our reluctance to believe him so incompetent a murderer as to leave so many direct clues.

At that point, Cornelius interrupted. "Ah, I should share a piece of information that is commonly available in certain circles, but perhaps unknown to you: Blaine's sexual tastes tend toward biting. Ms. Andrews, perhaps you're not familiar with that particular preference, as a newly turned vampire?"

"It's been explained, but I'm not sure I understand why that type of information would be gossip." Cornelius's eyes narrowed at the word "gossip." I mentally shrugged. Men and their refusal to accept the truth. Information, gossip—it was all context. "Is it prohibited or socially unacceptable or something?"

"No," Cornelius said. "It's more a totality of the circumstances that makes Blaine's behavior noteworthy. As one who does not partake, you may be unaware, but it's impossible for a vampire to consume blood infected with the vampire virus without becoming violently ill. Additionally, Blaine holds a certain political viewpoint that esteems vampires above all other enhanced creatures, most especially as partners. And yet he has a known proclivity for biting during sex."

I was floored. Also appalled and confused.

Wembley must have seen my confusion, because he

said, "Blaine isn't the type to self-harm, so he's having sex with non vamps. You understand?"

"Whoa—back up. Forget the biting. Go back to the blatant prejudice." Gladys had hinted...but this was another level entirely. "How can we have a candidate for CEO—that's basically our mayor, right?—who thinks one kind of enhanced person is superior to all others?"

Everyone in the room stared at me, even Bradley.

"Okay, I realized how silly that sounded after I said it. But I think you know what I mean."

Bradley, bless him, said he did.

"Back to my original point," Cornelius said. "It directly contradicts his political platform—the one that Ms. Andrews finds so abhorrent—to date, marry, or consort with anyone not a vampire."

"But doing so wouldn't be crippling in terms of the selection," Alex said. It wasn't a question, so Alex must have been up on some of this news.

"It's embarrassing for him, but as Alex says, not crippling," Cornelius said. "If your frame-up theory holds, the knowledge of his particular preferences could have been useful." He clasped his hands together and leaned forward. "And that brings me to a much more important point. Blaine's activities, barring proof that he's murdered Tabitha, are not crippling because Blaine faces very little opposition. The founding families are simply not nominating candidates. Blaine and Oscar still stand alone, unless you've changed your mind and are going to accept the nomination, Alex?"

"No, but I'm thinking it might be helpful to spread around the word that I am, so I told Blaine and Oscar I would be. If someone's trying to tamper with the selection, then I might be perceived as a threat."

"Someone—you mean if Oscar's behind the tampering?" Even I could do that math. Two guys running for office, one is the target of a frame-up, leaving the other free to win.

"Yes, Oscar is the only other candidate," Alex said, "But it's hard for me to believe he's behind such a scheme."

I also balked at the thought. "I don't know much about him, but I got used-car-salesman vibes from him, not mastermind."

Cornelius looked less certain. "As the only other candidate, he should jump to the top of your suspect list. But there is another possibility. Several days stand between today and the affirmation of nominations. Until Friday's ceremony, nominations are open, and a dark horse candidate could emerge."

Wembley finally joined us in the living room. He sat in the armchair nearest the kitchen then said, "Now that's a theory I can get behind. Tear down the candidates, prevent additional nominations, and then swoop in as the only viable candidate in the last moments before confirmation of the nominations. We need an inside track to the founding families. Do you have a replacement for Tabitha in mind?"

"Not immediately, no." Cornelius's voice sharpened. "There's a reluctance to accept the position for obvious reasons."

"How about her research?" Alex asked. "Or at least names and contact information."

"I've got Anton pulling together what he can find.

I had visions of spending the next few days behind a desk, calling parts distant, and being stonewalled, all while mean Mr. Clean breathed down my neck. Probably what real detective work was like, minus Anton's inquisition-inspired management style.

"I can help," Bradley said.

And immediately my visions morphed to Bradley calling parts distant...Bradley speaking on the phone to complete strangers. My temples throbbed.

"Give me what data you have," Bradley told Cornelius. "I can put together files on the families, check for recent alterations in patterns, criminal histories, and weaknesses a blackmailer might exploit."

So much more reasonable than my visions of him chatting with strangers by phone. But he didn't have the time—or shouldn't take the time. "What about your project?"

He blinked. "When can you deliver the data?" he asked Cornelius.

Cornelius considered for several seconds before responding. "I'll have Anton bring you the information we have. He should be here in fifteen minutes."

Bradley agreed to start right away. To me, he said, "I'll finish my project a day later. They'll wait and I'll still make lots of money. Don't worry so much, Mallory."

I didn't worry too much. I worried just the right amount.

Cornelius turned his full attention to me. "So, Ms. Andrews—Mallory—how is your investigation into Bitsy Jenkins disappearance proceeding? I assume you've considered that she is a suspect in this murder, given the use of her car as the disposal site."

The air started to sting my too-wide eyes. Bitsy, how could I have forgotten? And I was the worst investigator ever.

"She's been busy helping me with the Waters murder." Alex said. A little too casually, he added, "She has a connection with the lead investigator, Detective Ruiz."

"Ah, yes." Cornelius brushed an invisible piece of lint off his jacket. "Our possible inside man in the local police force. Has he come any closer to making a decision?"

When I just stared back at him, he elaborated. "Has he decided to become a friend of the Society and sign our non-disclosure agreement, or does he prefer the memory-wipe option?"

Since we were more on the cusp of dating than at the point of confiding big secrets, I didn't have a clue. "Ah. I'm not sure. We haven't discussed it."

"Perhaps you should take time from your busy schedule, and do so. I've already provided him with an extension. If he doesn't decide, I'll decide for him." Cornelius leaned forward. He was halfway across the room, and it was still intimidating. "And sort out what's happened to little Bitsy Jenkins. If I receive another visit from Gladys Pepperman, it will not be appreciated."

I nodded.

Cornelius stood up, signaling an end to the meeting. "Bradley, your data will arrive shortly. We appreciate you making this case a priority. Alex, I'll expect an update on Oscar and Blaine as you gather information. Should a candidate be responsible for the death, I need to know immediately. Conclusive evidence of tampering will result in removal from the selection process. Given the time sensitive nature of the process, I need to start the paperwork immediately."

"Ah…" I raised my hand, Bradley-style, because my brain was about to explode and I wanted him to stop speaking. "Is Tabitha's death not a worse crime? An executable crime?" I hoped so, because I'd had more than enough of the Society's backward and upside-down laws.

Alex stood up and shot me a warning look. "I'll handle this one, Cornelius. And I'll get you an update on the autopsy when Star gets back to me with the final results."

He and Cornelius walked to the front door while I sat in

my chair and wondered how I was a part of such a messed up world.

Go ahead, kill whoever you like, but don't dare interfere with our election. *That* was my new community, my new government. At first it had been disturbing, but now it was just depressing. I wasn't sure I was up to the challenge of discovering yet more of the Society unwashed linen.

17

NOT QUITE DEAD

Bradley got up, looked at me with an unreadable expression, then hoofed it to the study.

I couldn't blame him. He had more than one pressing deadline, and even I wouldn't want to talk to me right now.

Alex and Cornelius's voices drifting in from the hall, but I couldn't make out specific words. For all I knew, they were chatting like two old farmers about the weather. Or maybe how they could commit murder and get away with it—because that seemed to be acceptable in the Society.

"It's more complicated than you're seeing right now." Wembley stood up and headed to the kitchen. "Juice? Juice makes everything better."

"Juice won't make this better. Not even your awesome vegan cheese soup will make this better."

"Come on," he called from the kitchen. "You'll feel better if you have some food in you."

I heard the fridge door open and hopped up to see what emerged. When I walked into the kitchen, I found one of my standard vegan supplement shakes and three new varieties of juice on the kitchen table.

"I thought it was time to get a little funky, so I went with some green choices this time."

I melted into the chair in front of the display of goodies. "You're too good to me. I don't deserve you."

Wembley sat down across from me. "You don't, but you do realize I haven't paid rent since I moved in? If I stop plying you with decent food, you might realize and start charging me."

"That is an excellent point." I twisted the cap off my first experimental green drink. "Why do they call these smoothies? They're just juice, right?"

Wembley scratched his jaw then sat back in his chair. "I think the question you really want to ask is, how can someone get away with murder?"

Alex came into the kitchen. "The short answer is that they won't. Finish your juice. There's been a development on the Bitsy front. And wake up that lazy hound dog. He's coming with us."

"Boone isn't lazy. He has good taste. He was avoiding Cornelius." Proof positive of my statement appeared in the form of Boone. Now that Cornelius was gone, he was ready for some food or ear rubs, whichever we were handing out.

"You like Cornelius, Mallory." Alex rubbed the hound's ears. "Not right now, but usually. Don't forget that. And drink your juice. We're on the clock again."

I finished green juice concoction number one and gave Wembley a thumbs-up. I didn't ask about Bitsy, because I was afraid I knew. I didn't want to hear she was dead. Not right now. I could hear that after I drank my shakes. My hand shook slightly as I uncapped the second bottle.

"So, as I was saying before I was so rudely interrupted, the killer isn't getting away with murder." Wembley motioned for me to keep drinking. "You know from past experience that exposure to human eyes is taken very seriously by the Society. The body was left in an open trunk in a public place with puncture wounds. That's nothing if not exposure to human eyes. For that alone, this killer is getting the rope."

"This one's good, too." I toasted him with green drink number two. "If that's the case, why didn't Cornelius say that?"

"Because there might be mitigating circumstances surrounding Tabitha's death, but tampering with the selection means exclusion as a candidate. Period. He was just prioritizing. Even Wembley agrees, and he can't stand Cornelius."

Wembley nodded. "Don't trust him as far as I can throw him."

I'd finished the second bottle and started the third. I took a sip, made a face, and said, "Nope."

Wembley snatched it and took a sip. With puckered lips, he said, "My bad."

Alex's phone pinged, and after glancing at it, he said, "We need to go."

I left the last juice with Wembley, but grabbed a shake out of the fridge. Finally, I asked, suspecting the answer, "She's dead, isn't she?"

Alex started to reply, stopped, then said, "Not exactly."

"I'm sorry, how is someone 'not exactly' dead?"

Wembley crossed his arms. "I'm with Mallory on this one."

Alex gritted his teeth. "All right, then—she's alive. But so far as Francis can tell, nothing that was Bitsy remains. I can't say more than that, because I don't know. She's conscious now, though, so we can try to talk to her. She's at the Society's headquarters. Francis just brought her in from her apartment."

I felt sick. When Alex had briefed me, he'd said her apartment had been checked and there were signs that she'd been away for several days. We'd been busy today, so I hadn't had time to go by myself. I should have made time.

I clutched the shake with numb fingers. "How long was she there?"

"Francis suspects late last night, early this morning, but he's guessing. She's in no state to have made her own way home, so she was either dumped, or whatever happened to her took place in her apartment." Alex shook his head. "You should stay here. I'll interview her."

"No." I stood up and almost stepped on Boone. He'd moved to sit next to me, but I hadn't noticed. I rubbed his long, silky ears. "What did you need Boone for? Oh, the apartment. You want him to check it out just in case the killer was there."

"I did." Alex said, watching me. "Okay, if you're sure. Wembley, if you can give us a lift to Bits, Baubles, and Toadstools, my car is there. Mandy picked it up from the hotel earlier."

Wembley nodded, then said to me, "And I'll grab your spare long line for Boone, since all his equipment is in the Jeep."

I grabbed my purse with the saliva samples, stared at the shake on the table, and then shoved it in my purse as well.

Bradley barely looked up when I told him we were going out. I doubted he'd want to miss his appointment this evening with the retirees, so it looked like he might be attending on his own after all.

A few minutes later, Alex, Wembley, Boone, and I were

loaded up in the van. The drive was short, since Society headquarters was only a few miles away from my house.

There wasn't any chatter, no talking case theories or hypothesizing what had happened to Bitsy. We were all too worried about what we'd find. Wembley dropped Alex and I, then said he was heading back to the house to keep Bradley company. I wasn't sure if that was code for keeping an eye on Bradley, or if he wanted to avoid the meeting Alex and I were about to have with Bitsy. Either way, I understood.

I walked through the doors of Bits, Baubles, and Toadstools with Boone on my heels. I didn't even notice the new merchandise, just rushed through the retail area with a quick wave at Mandy and headed straight for the door in the back marked Employees Only. I didn't know the new code—it changed frequently—so I had to wait for Alex to catch up.

I stopped at the door and watched him approach. Alex was usually quick on his feet, much quicker than me. He'd also not been in a particular rush to leave my house, all things considered.

As he punched in the code, I leaned in close to him. "You know what's wrong with her."

His hand hovered over the keypad. "No."

"You suspect."

He nodded, punched the last key, and opened the door. He held it open with one arm and waited for me to walk through. He wouldn't meet my gaze.

He knew, and it upset him.

I stepped through the doorway then paused. As he stepped next to me, I grabbed his hand and held on tight. He hesitated, then walked down the hall, my hand in his.

We dropped Boone in his office, then passed by the

lounge, then the hallway that led to Cornelius's office. Finally, we came to a door. I'd never been through this door before. I was pretty sure this was where they took the prisoners to record their witch-induced confessions. Probably where the executions happened.

"You good?" I asked.

"No." He looked down at me. "But thanks for asking."

I gave his hand a final squeeze and let go.

He opened the door, and this time he walked through first. I followed close behind him, because the hallway was too narrow for us to pass side by side. He went a few feet, paused at a door to the right just long enough to knock quietly, and then entered without waiting for a response.

"Francis," he said as he stepped through.

I followed behind and entered a room bathed in sunlight. This certainly wasn't the execution wing, since anything to do with killing people would be an interior room with no windows. One concern knocked off my long list.

It took a second for my eyes to adjust to the natural light, but then I saw that the room was almost empty. A twin bed and a folding chair placed next to it were the only furniture. Francis had risen from the chair as we'd entered. His usual cheerful expression was absent, and in its place was a strained, pinched look.

I turned to the bed. A woman lay there on top of a thin comforter. She had on jeans and a cute knit top. Mid-twenties, medium brown hair, lightly tanned, trim, an almost boyish figure. She looked peaceful. I looked closer. Not peaceful, blank. Until her fangs descended, and then she looked hungry.

"Watch out," Francis said. He pulled a bottle of blood

from a cooler at the end of the bed. He propped her up and encouraged her to take a few sips.

Her fangs receded and the blank look returned.

Francis carefully lowered her back down to the bed. "Ever since she woke up, she's been like that: zoned out and then all of a sudden her fangs drop. She's half starved and I can't get her to drink to satiation, so I think she'll keep doing this."

Very quietly, I said, "What happens if you don't feed her?"

He turned to show me a partially healed wound on his forearm. It was ragged, not neat like the punctures I'd seen on Tabitha. "You don't need to whisper. She's not bothered by voices. She doesn't respond at all."

I'm not sure why I felt the need to try, but I did. "Bitsy—"

"Strip her." Alex didn't look away from Bitsy's prone form, but he must have been talking to Francis.

Without hesitation, Francis started to remove her clothes. He reached for her top, but I stopped him with a hand on his arm.

"Are you sure?" I asked Alex. When he nodded, I said, "I'll do it. I know she doesn't know what's happening, but... just... I'll do it."

I tugged the bottom of her shirt up, stopped just short of her bra, and hesitated because she was completely limp. Her eyes were open, apparently seeing, but no one was home. It was eerie. I shook my head and kept tugging till her shirt was off.

I was unbuttoning her pants when Alex said, "Stop. Francis, help me flip her over."

He could have done it alone, but between the two of them they carefully, gently turned her over. And then I saw exactly what Alex was looking for.

A series of symbols covered her lower back. The flesh was shiny, like a newly healed wound. Like a newly healed burn. Someone had branded her.

18

HOW UNVAMPY CAN A VAMP GIRL BE?

"Holy hell," Francis said, which was exactly what I was thinking. He pulled out his phone and snapped a pic. "I'm sending this to Cornelius."

The three of us stared at the poor woman's back for I didn't know how long. Finally, Alex said, "We have to burn them off her."

"Wait—what?" I yelled. I quickly turned to see if I'd upset her, but she remained unmoving, staring blankly. I didn't want to say it in front of Francis, but those marks on Bitsy's back bore a remarkable resemblance to the tattoos covering much of Alex's chest and back. And I wasn't sure he could be objective, knowing as I did how ashamed he was of the marks covering his body.

Francis's face had a pinched, tight look, but in a firm voice he asked, "With magic or mundane flame?"

Alex pinched the bridge of his nose. "I don't know. Magic might be a problem—flame, I guess."

"Doing this will help her?" I asked. "It will bring her memories, her personality back?"

"I don't know, but they can't stay. Whoever burned her used the symbols to bind her to them. To control her."

Bitsy lay on her stomach, her head turned to face us, eyes open but unseeing.

"Alex, no one is controlling her now," I said.

"That's because he burned her out." He squeezed his eyes shut. "Trust me. Even though he's not controlling her now, we need to destroy the tie. And to destroy the tie, you have to destroy the symbols." He paused a heartbeat, and added, "I'm pretty sure."

"You're pretty sure? Not to be fussy or anything, Alex, but this is a woman who isn't able to speak for herself. Be sure."

A light knock sounded, and Cornelius entered the room. "We have the woman, but no clue as to where she's been or how she came to be this way. Ms. Andrews, I'm afraid you've underwhelmed me."

I was not in the mood to be intimidated, not this time. We were about to light this woman's flesh on fire, and someone needed to have their head in the game. "Thanks for that, but we have bigger concerns right now, like burning a woman without her consent. What do you know about these symbols?"

Cornelius turned to Alex. "Any thoughts?"

"I can't read them. Have a look yourself, but it's not a language I recognize."

Francis looked up from Bitsy to the two men and said, "I should run an errand, shouldn't I?"

Cornelius nodded, and then clapped Francis on the shoulder as he walked by and said, "Your discretion is much appreciated." Once Francis was gone, Cornelius said, "Superstitions still persist, even though alchemic knowledge is no longer forbidden." He was looking at me, but it felt like he was talking to Alex.

Once we tied up this case, I'd be doing some research on alchemy.

Alex and Cornelius moved closer to Bitsy and examined the scars on her lower back. I, however, kept a close watch on her face. If her fangs dropped again, I didn't want anyone shredded before we could get her fed.

"I'm not sure what they are," Cornelius said. "I don't recognize them, but I don't have your expertise. It's the same binding ceremony? Otherwise, I don't know why Ms. Andrews is going on about burning."

"Indelible symbols, the placement on her torso, all the signs of burnout—I think it's the binding ceremony."

"Newbie here," I said, my gaze flickering between them and Bitsy. "What does a binding ceremony do?"

Alex looked at me, really looked. It was like a physical connection between us. "Cornelius has recently been helping me research a way to undo a mistake I made a long time ago. The symbols on my body bind me to specific demons, spirits, and elementals, and those bindings give me limited power over them and those under their dominion."

Wow. That explained a few things. I wondered if Cornelius knew the street could run both ways, that Alex could—in moments of extreme weakness—be taken over by those creatures. If he didn't, I wasn't about to be the one to tell him. I had more loyalty to Alex than Cornelius, any day, every day.

With me so intent on Alex's revelation and Cornelius unaware of Bitsy's regular feeding requirement, we must have missed it when her fangs initially dropped. Because one minute I was staring into Alex's baby blues as he shared his deep, dark secrets, and the next I had a rabid vamp clinging to my arm.

Rabid vamp, hanging off my arm. Ouch.

My impulse was to fight, jerk my arm away, smash her over the head with anything handy—but Francis *had*, and those ragged punctures had looked wicked painful.

Alex moved toward me, probably to yank Bitsy off me and create all sorts of not-neat puncture wounds, so I held my hand out to stop him.

He looked comically surprised.

Cornelius was just a hair slower. I didn't have another free hand, so I placed my body between him and Bitsy.

Except none of that was possible, because I was the slowest person in the room. As that realization dawned, the world returned to its normal speed.

"What are you doing?" Alex said at the same time that Cornelius said, "How is that possible?"

Adrenaline was my friend. I'd forgotten about that.

"Stressed-out superspeed, remember? I get wigged out, big adrenaline rush—or vamp rush—and I can move really fast for about two seconds—not literally, I've never timed it. But let's chat later and remove vamp fangs now."

"I was trying to when you shoved me in the chest," Alex said with a slightly panicked edge.

"I'm fine, Alex. It just feels weird. One of you hold her while the other one pries her jaws loose. Just watch it with the ripping. Francis's arm didn't look so hot."

Quicker than a blink, Cornelius secured Bitsy. It looked suspiciously like some type of wrestling hold. Cornelius might have been watching a little too much WWE.

I moved out of Alex's way so he could reach Bitsy, stumbled, and almost fell. "Okay, now you can hurry. I might be a little lightheaded."

"Mallory, I swear—" But he clenched his jaw and very carefully pried loose the leech that had attached herself to me. As soon as he did, her fangs receded.

"Ick. That is so gross." I clamped my left hand over the two neat puncture marks she'd left. So much for vamp saliva healing. Since I didn't drink people juice, I didn't know how it worked, but I vaguely remembered something about licking the wound to seal it.

I wasn't licking anything, and no way I'd let leech girl near my arm again. Two holes in my arm wasn't looking so bad in comparison.

"Well, that's unfortunate for you, dear," Cornelius said, "but I suspect Bitsy Jenkins will be in a much worse place. In case you've forgotten, vamps can't consume vamp blood."

Bitsy had closed her eyes as she'd fed from my arm. Now, as Cornelius held her, she stretched her neck, licked her lips, and made a small sound of satisfaction, suspiciously like a purr. Then she opened her heavy-lidded eyes and said, "Where am I?"

And then she passed out.

After a few seconds in which no one moved or even breathed, Cornelius cleared his throat. Then he did it again.

Alex grabbed her feet, Cornelius her shoulders, and they placed her on the bed. After a brief examination, Cornelius pronounced her deeply asleep.

Alex said, "Not a word of what happened leaves this room."

Cornelius shared a glance with Alex and said, "Agreed."

"Not a word of what?" Vampires could move fast all the time. The fact that my brand of fast was limited to highly charged moments, and even then only erratically so, wasn't something I was keen to share, but it also wasn't big, dark secret material.

Cornelius gestured to the now gently snoring Bitsy. "She can't drink vamp blood." His tone became clipped and very British. "You are most certainly a vampire."

I almost said, "sort of," but Cornelius's tone prevented me. He was deadly serious.

"More than that." Alex couldn't take his eyes away from Bitsy. "Look at her. Five minutes ago, she was burned out. Now she's sleeping."

Cornelius touched my arm. Briefly, but still—Cornelius never touched me. "People aren't puppets to be manipulated like dolls. Bending a person's mind, their will, and in Bitsy's case her magic, breaks something deep in the human psyche. Or maybe it's the soul. I'm not certain. I *do* know it's called burnout and looks exactly like Bitsy before she fed from you."

I wasn't sure what they were saying...except I was. My blood didn't make her sick, and maybe it made her better. "But she's a vamp. Do you know anything about burnout with vamps? They're—we're—probably different."

A light knock on the door precluded a response, and then Francis came in carrying a few bottles of blood, a knit blanket, and fresh towels.

What would real vampires do without that nifty witch invention, the stasis bottle? Inside these bewitched bottles, blood stayed in its newly drawn, unclotted form for up to thirty days. Yuck, but yet awesome.

"Didn't want to run out of blood." Francis stopped quite suddenly in the middle of the room, then he turned slowly toward Bitsy. "Is she snoring?"

I waited for someone else to say something, because I hardly had the knowledge or cred to pull off some massive fib.

Turned out, it wasn't necessary. A huge grin spread across Francis's face, and he said, "It worked. Whatever you guys did, it worked."

I nonchalantly clasped my hands behind my back, hiding my newly acquired bite marks.

"We don't know that. We'll have to see what state she's in when she's fully conscious." Cornelius eyed the sleeping woman. "Give her a few hours, then wake her up—but be sure to have backup on hand when you do."

I nudged Alex with my toe. "Put her shirt back on."

He didn't look enthused by the prospect. "I'm not sure we should risk waking her."

"Better she should wake up half naked in a room with strangers? Besides, I doubt a brass band would wake her up at this point."

It took some doing, unconscious people were surprisingly hard to dress, but Alex managed it. When he was done, he stepped between me and Francis, shielding my top-secret bite from view, and hustled me out the door. Before he shut it, he said, "A word Cornelius?"

We waited in the hall while Cornelius gave Francis a few more instructions.

When he emerged in the hall, he asked, "My office?"

"No time. We've got Boone in mine. We're headed to Bitsy's apartment with him to see if he can identify anyone, besides Bitsy, in the apartment. I just needed to tell you..." Alex rubbed his neck. "The scars on her back are gone."

Uh-oh. Vamps healed. It happened. But if she was going to heal those scars, she'd have already done it.

The two men shared a look, and Cornelius said, "Not a word. Check in after the hound's been through the apartment. Have him check the parking lot, as well. It's well-trafficked, but you never know what odd scent will register as familiar."

Alex nodded, and we left. It was all hush-hush, on the sly, feeling, beginning with Cornelius's visit to my house, then the bare room in the back of the warehouse, aka Bits, Baubles, and Toadstools, aka Society headquarters, and now our quiet, hurried escape from the building. Alex and I didn't normally roll this way.

I shook my head, but trudged along behind as we headed to the office. We stopped long enough to pick up Boone and grab a few extra water bottles out of Alex's fridge, then we headed out to the car.

Boone seemed to sense the tension, because he stuck especially close.

When we got out to the parking lot, Alex pointed to a sleek black car. It was one James Bond move too far, and I giggled.

"*That's* your personal car?"

It looked like a family car had mated with a car from the future and had a luxurious black baby car.

"One of them." Alex opened the back door for Boone.

I opened the door to a dash full of tech. "It's more computer than car." Alex quirked an eyebrow at me, so I amended my evaluation. "Okay, that's a minor exaggeration. Boone, do not drool on anything that looks electronic." I sat down on the buttery leather seat. "Or anything that looks expensive."

Alex snorted.

"Hey, I tried."

We started to roll, and I grabbed at the armrest...until I realized we weren't rolling but backing up. Alex pulled out of the parking lot and zipped down the road. Since I still couldn't hear an engine, I figured it had to be electric and not a hybrid. "Tesla?"

He nodded.

"It just seems like a strange choice. It's basically a

commuter car with a huge backseat. You're not hiding 2.4 kids that I don't know about, are you?"

He gave me a strange look. "No kids. But the trunk is great for toting around dead bodies."

I winced.

"Too soon?" he asked.

"Yeah. For future reference, less than twenty-four hours is always too soon."

Maybe it was the casual tone of our conversation, maybe escaping a tense situation, maybe just the entertaining thought of Alex enjoying the stench of bloodhound every time he got in his car for the next week, but something eased inside me—and out popped an idea.

"Alex, I believe I've had a not insignificant thought." And I flashed him my brightest smile of the day.

19

SLEIGHT OF HAND

"Do I need to pull over and take notes, or can I keep driving to Bitsy's?" Alex asked.

"I'm serious. I've had a revelation. A moment of true enlightenment. And you, with your sarcasm, might be putting a dent in my happy." Which was actually pretty awesome news. It meant I had some happy to dent. It had been a rough day.

"You've got my almost full attention."

Since he was driving, I figured that was good enough.

"This case is all about sleight of hand, manipulation, and playing from the shadows. Blaine's not the guy, right? I mean, as much I want him to be the guy because I don't want him to be CEO, we're agreed that he's probably not the guy."

"He may not be old, but he's also not newly turned. And he's not a complete idiot, so I'll agree that, yes, I do have my doubts." Alex glanced at me. "He has enough skill to have prevented the accumulation of evidence we're seeing."

"I know. We're supposed to follow the evidence, but—"

Boone caught my eye as he rested his head on the console in between the front seats. He wasn't drooling. Yet.

Alex glanced down at the hound. "It's fine. I'll just get it cleaned if I need to. You were saying, sleight of hand?"

I ticked off on my fingers the various manipulations we'd encountered. "The text. Sent from Blaine's phone, but Blaine claims not by him. Whoever did send it had early knowledge of the murder. The maid. She works for him, has access to his phone, and then mysteriously tries to speak with us when we visit. Maybe she's having regrets? Or has discovered a belated sense of loyalty to Blaine?"

Alex turned at a major intersection. The apartment was only a few streets farther. "Assuming she was hired by the killer and that person is not Blaine, then it's more likely she was afraid of the killer coming after her to tie up loose ends."

"Either way, it's all manipulation and sleight of hand. I think someone knew about his relationship with Tabitha and set her up to eat that amethyst knowing Blaine would drink her blood and inadvertently kill her."

"Yes, I'll agree that the intimate details of Blaine's sex life weren't actually so intimate. And enough people were aware of his tastes to make it possible the information was used against him. But you're not giving me any new evidence. We knew all of this before."

I frowned at him. "I'm giving you a thread that ties everything together. Okay, here's another one. You remember what Star said when she found the stone in Tabitha? About someone tricking her into eating it?" I spread my hands wide. "Manipulation, trickery."

I tried to grab the thought I'd had before, when we'd been at the mortuary.

"Still not evidence."

"Okay, then there's Bitsy's binding, the ultimate in manipulation. What was she doing during those missing days? As for her car, we know she wasn't driving it last night, because your spirit informants told you a *man* was driving the car. And why leave the body in an easily identifiable car —with the trunk partially open, no less—other than to intentionally mislead us? This guy is pointing the finger everywhere but at himself."

"Lots of theories, very little evidence," Alex pointed out. "But to support your argument of a master manipulator, I'll admit that my gut says Bitsy was intended to retrieve Tabitha's body and to remove the stone, but our guy's plan failed when she burned out sooner than he expected." He gave Boone's ear a scratch. "Any chance you can tell us a *when* rather than a *who*, hound dog?"

Boone groaned and sighed simultaneously.

I leaned to the side so I could look him in his houndy face. "You think you can figure out what time Bitsy came back to the apartment after being gone a few days?"

He picked his head up off the center consul, and his ears perked up.

"I'm calling that a yes." I gave Alex an assessing look. "So, are you buying the general theme: work from the shadows, manipulate, misdirect?"

"Almost. You've forgotten the incident with the brakes. That doesn't exactly fit your pattern."

I could feel a growl burbling in my throat. Not because Alex didn't agree, but because he was right. "Attacking the investigators on the case does seem pretty direct." It stood out as both a more direct attack and significantly less effective one. "Do you suppose it was supposed to kill us?"

Alex looked offended.

I bit back a grin. "I'm not criticizing your driving."

"Good thing," he murmured.

"I'm saying, what was the intent behind the sabotage? I can't remember the exact details, but I do remember you telling me when I was first turned that a car crash could kill me now as easily as before." I bit my lip, but the specifics of that conversation eluded me. "I got the distinct impression at the time that you were trying to scare me into being careful—and *not* that car accidents were a big paranormal people killer."

"Probably correct. You can be reckless sometimes." He sounded distracted, but he was also slowing down to pull into a small apartment complex, Bitsy's apartment complex. "It's frustrating. You don't always recognize your mortality. Newly turned vamps can be careless that way."

I looked at him. It was like he was chattering to fill the silence. Alex didn't chatter, and he was definitely distracted.

He pulled into an empty space, and when he put the car in park, Boone bounced to the door and stared out the window. And now there were nose prints on the window glass.

"I think he's ready to go." It was good to see one of us fully charged and ready to tackle an investigation, because I suddenly realized how tired *I* was. Being Bitsy's personal blood bank had taken more of a toll than I'd realized. After the initial lightheadedness I hadn't noticed anything. But now I was definitely feeling tired.

Alex lifted a finger. "Hang on." Then he picked up his phone and called someone.

Now didn't seem like the time for a chat, but if he was gonna gab on the phone then I was tanking up on fluids. I retrieved one of the bottles of water we'd brought along and twisted the cap off. I really should have been guzzling water during the drive. I seemed to get dehydrated easily, and, with Bitsy's pillaging of my bodily fluids, I was in more of a deficit than usual.

I looked out the passenger window as I drank. I could see most of the units from inside the car. The complex wasn't very big, maybe fifteen or twenty units.

"Star, thanks for answering. Have you had a chance to look at Mallory's Grand Cherokee? Yes, I do realize the mortuary is still open. Yes, I remember you saying you wouldn't look at it until after closing. No, I haven't lost my mind, and I do value your time." Alex sighed. "Star, please, will you go have a look? Just a quick look, not a full work up. Yes, I agree to your terms. Thank you."

After he hung up, he squeezed the phone. For a moment, I thought he was going to break it. Then he loosened his grip, and set the phone gently on the dash.

Several seconds went by and he didn't say anything or make a move to exit the car.

I drank some more water.

Boone whined.

Alex still didn't look any closer to getting out of the car.

I finished the bottle and chucked it on the floorboard.

Alex didn't comment, didn't move.

I considered my options. Silence—an awkward, ever-expanding silence—or not. I lasted about a second before I said, "So we're waiting until Star calls back."

"Yes." He kept staring out the front of the window.

That didn't work. From chitchat to silence, it was weird. "Is everything okay?"

He nodded.

"It's hard for me to envision you two dating."

And that did it. He finally turned away from whatever distant thought had absorbed him and looked at me. "We didn't date. We lived together. It was more like an ill-conceived marriage than a romance." He rubbed his fore-head and sighed. "That's not fair. I'm just frustrated with her recently. We've had an excellent business relationship for years, and all of a sudden...it's just different."

"But she's still happy to take your money."

He gave me a wry smile. "Yes."

And together we both said, "Four kids."

I shook my head. "Her fixation on that education fund is comical."

"Actually..." Alex tilted his head. "It's an excuse. I know that she loves the parts of her life that she thinks of as normal—being a mother and a wife, running her husband's family business—but she misses the magic. Worse, she feels bad about missing it, so she uses the kids' college funds as an excuse to take witch gigs."

"Really?" An entire side of Star, I'd never have guessed at, the Stephanie side. "What does her husband have to say about that?"

His lips twitched. "Couldn't care less. As long as she's happy, he's thrilled. He adores her. They're perfect for each other." He leaned back in his seat. "It's funny. She gets a kick out of running the mortuary now, but she took it on origi-nally so her husband could work in a different field. He never liked the work, but he refused to close the place down because it was a family business. Star just took it over, kicked him out, and told him to do what he loved."

"They sound so...sweet." I surprised myself when I said it. "In a weird way, since we're talking funeral homes and witch magic."

But Alex chuckled. "Weirdly sweet is a good way to describe them." More seriously, he said, "Something's changed recently. Between Star and me, not her husband."

The phone rang, which was a good thing, because I

suspected the change was in Alex. And if we hadn't been interrupted, I might have said so.

He waited a ring before picking it up, and when he spoke, his voice was brisk and business-like. "What did you find? You're sure?" He cursed, but it seemed more frustration than anything else. "Sorry, yes, thank you. I do appreciate your time." He looked at me and said, "Yes, I'll tell her. No, I won't tell her that." He tapped the phone to end the call.

"So?" I scooted to the edge of my seat. "What did she find?"

"Tangwystl in the backseat. Star moved her to an unprotected area of the funeral home, so you should be able to call her to you now. Star's protections would have trapped her there."

"That's a relief. I thought she was in a snit because I forgot about her. But what about the brakes?"

He hesitated and then said, "I'm sorry about that."

I waited for the punchline. I'm sorry, but she couldn't find anything. I'm sorry, but...

"When you said the sabotage of the brakes stood out as different from the rest of the evidence in the case, and that it wasn't intended to kill, something bothered me." He paused, shifted in his seat, then said, "Star's just confirmed my suspicions. I think the person who did this was a girl I was seeing briefly, and that she targeted you because we spend a lot of time together." He looked at me like he wanted to say more, but then his lips thinned, he nodded, and then got out of the car.

An ex? We had a near-death—sort of—experience, because of a jealous ex? If he hadn't looked upset about it, I might have yelled. No, I didn't yell these days. Chewed him out, that was more reasonable.

Boone whined and gave me a mournful look when I didn't exit with sufficient speed.

"I get it, you've been very patient. But you have to admit, he's annoying. And his exes, legion in number that they are, are even more annoying."

Boone whined at me and then pressed his nose against the glass, making yet another smudgy snot print on Alex's car.

"You're right. Time to stop obsessing over ex-lovers and get rolling. We'll ponder the mysteries of Alex some other time." I grabbed the long line I'd dropped on the floor-boards and slid out of the car.

Before I shut the door, I retrieved one of the sample jars from my bag and put it on the hood.

I opened the door for Boone and attached the lead. He jumped out and waited for me, but despite his polite behavior he was clearly excited. He practically vibrated with suppressed energy. "What's the apartment number?"

Alex met me at the front of the car. "Five. Are we good?"

"Do I care that some gal you're shagging didn't quite try to kill me? Not thrilled about that, but I'm guessing you didn't encourage her to do it."

"In fact, I didn't encourage her at all, in any way, to do anything. And she's not just a 'gal,' or there wouldn't have been a problem. She's a witch."

I felt a little sorry for that witch. If I had hot monkey sex with Alex, I probably wouldn't want to give him up either. But not too sorry, because I liked having functioning brakes on my car. "Do I know her?"

"I don't think so. You know *about* her. She's the woman I was on a dinner date with when you called emergency response that first time."

I lifted my index finger. "The one and only time I've ever

called emergency response or ever will." I looked down at Boone. He stood next to me, ears perked, tail up, ready to go. Then he lifted his head and gave me that mournful, poor, neglected hound look. "You are a gentleman among hounds, Boone. I know you're excited to get started."

He made a high-pitched sound that was somewhere between a yip and a whine.

I pulled out the Ziploc bag with Star's hair and scent pad first. I showed it to him and said, "Star says hello. The nice witch lady who does all sorts of magical forensics for us, that one."

Boone huffed out an impatient breath.

"Sorry, she was worried that having touched everything, you'd want to know which was her scent."

Alex cleared his throat. "Are you sure he understands everything you say?"

Boone turned to Alex and gave him the evil eye.

I couldn't help a smirk. "I think that says it all. Whatever djinn magic he got from Celia seems to be sticking."

Boone's ears drooped at the sound of Celia's name. She was his former handler and partner, killed by some murderous wenches. Celia was also the one who'd imbued him with the ability to not only understand humans, but in limited ways to think like them.

"Ready for your target scent?" I asked.

He perked up again, and I presented him with the vamp saliva sample. Before I capped the glass jar again, I said, "Bad guy stink, got it?"

He chuffed hoarsely, his attempt at a quiet bark. We'd worked on that a bit. Most of his vocalizations tended to carry a few blocks. Not convenient for city living, or even 'burb living.

I handed the glass sample jar to Alex, and stuffed Star's

Ziploc in my pocket. If I lost it, I was pretty sure she'd know and witch justice would rain down upon me.

Once I had hold of Boone's long line and nothing else, he took off at a jog, zigzagging through the parking lot and letting out an occasional yip of excitement. He usually saved yipping for chasing critters in the yard. This much enthusiasm meant one of two things: either I didn't get him out to work often enough, or he'd hit bad-guy stink already.

20

SMOKE AND MIRRORS

As it turned out, I didn't need to find apartment number five, because Boone took us straight there. With great enthusiasm. He did a fly-by of one of Bitsy's neighbors as he trucked through the breezeway.

The guy made a snarky comment about how I should be walking the dog, not vice versa. Sometimes people were denser than their opposable thumbs and upright stance might lead one to believe.

I didn't have time to reply, because Boone bounded straight to the door of number five and, with a final yip, planted his front paws on the door.

He flung his head back, slobber flying, to grin at me in triumph.

"Sure, go ahead and gloat. We all know you have the best nose around."

Boone continued to grin, but he dropped down to stand with all four feet on the ground.

Alex joined us and said, "Just clearing up a little confusion. That gentleman will not be filing a complaint with the landlord."

I rolled my eyes. People were jerks. "Boone didn't even touch him."

Alex placed the back of his hand next to the locking mechanism on the door and the quiet sound of a deadbolt sliding followed. "Something along the lines of your leash being too long and your dog acting aggressively." He opened the door. "After you."

I don't know what I expected, but this wasn't it. There was nothing. Some furniture, yes, but no pictures, no small items, no personal touches, no clutter, no mail. If I had to guess, I'd even say the furnishings came with the apartment. Her place would make a great hotel room, but the fact that Bitsy called this home made me a little sad.

I trailed behind Boone as he nosed around the living room. "How long has she lived here?"

"A few months. She didn't attend orientation right away, which is how she ended up with Gladys's group." Alex scanned the room. "But you're right, it's sparse. Anyway, we can tick one question off the list. Whoever bit Tabitha was here. Now all we need is to identify who exactly that was, get a timeline, and then—"

A low rumbling noise cut him off. We looked at each other and then turned to Boone. The rumbling stopped.

"Seriously?" Alex looked at me. "He's saying whoever bit Tabitha was not here?" Boone's tail thumped against the ground. "What was all of the excitement for then?"

"I've learned it's better to ask, since Boone speaks English better than we speak hound." I turned my attention to Boone and found him grinning at me in what I liked to think was an approving way. "You found a scent to follow."

Tail thump.

I turned to Alex. "That's a yes."

He raised an eyebrow. "So I gathered. How about I let you handle the questions."

"Someone you know?" I asked.

He looked sad, but didn't dip his head, which meant "no," or wag his tail.

Alex shook his head. "While you interrogate the Nose, I'm going to have a look around." He pointed to the kitchen. "Starting there. Holler if you need anything."

"We've got this."

Since Boone wagged his tail, he figured we did, too.

"The scent's familiar?" Tail wag. "But not a person you've met before?" That question was greeted with a head tilt, not one of our prearranged signals.

I sat down on the sofa. "Have you encountered the scent before?" One half-hearted swish of his tail. "You've encountered a similar scent?" Tail wag.

"It's like that game, animal, vegetable or mineral, but with higher stakes," Alex called from the kitchen over the sound of clattering dishes.

Boone lifted his muzzle and let loose. "Wa-wooo!"

I squinted, like that was going to make the sound any quieter. "I think the landlord is getting a call after all, Alex."

He joined me in the living room. "What happened?"

I wasn't sure, but then I recalled the yipping noises that I'd taken for excitement. Combine that with Alex's comment, and I had a suspicion. "Animal, vegetable, mineral?" Tail wag and a huge doggy grin. "Animal?" Boone's tail wagged.

"Vegetable? Mineral?" I got a head dip for each.

I was an idiot. Or had been seriously magicked. Or both. "Oh, Alex. We've been had."

He rejoined me in the living room. "I don't follow."

"Exactly, that's the point. We're not meant to. What was I

saying before? It's all about deception, misdirection, trickery. Who excels at those things?" I turned to Boone and said, "Coyote?"

His tail wagged, and he chuffed out another muffled, but still very excited, bark.

I reached down to rub his ears and told him he was the best hound ever. But it was difficult to keep a light tone given how angry I was.

Alex's eyes narrowed. "But the only coyote we've got on the radar is Oscar. You think Oscar has something to do with this case? With the stones? With Tabitha's death? I know we said we'd keep him on the suspect list, but I just don't think so."

"I didn't either, Alex, even though he's a natural suspect. Even though Cornelius had concerns about him. And I think that if he's managed, through smoke and mirrors, to keep us looking away from him, that he's probably behind this all way back to Dyson's death. Killing the sitting CEO would be a great start to taking over the job, wouldn't it?"

"Oscar doesn't have the cash or the guile to manage something like this. And the stones? You think *Oscar* has the amethysts? Because I especially don't think he's capable of coordinating a plan that goes far enough back to kill the previous CEO."

"Listen to yourself. You just said you don't believe a man has the guile to be the killer, but he is the definition of guile. A coyote's stock in trade is persuasion and trickery." Alex was looking at me like I was nuts, so I tried a different tactic. "Do you remember when I met my first coyote, Becky Taylor? I asked you what their gifts were. Do you remember that?"

"Sure. I remember. I told you they make great magicians..." He frowned. "And con artists."

"Right. He's a con artist, Alex, and he's conned both of us into believing he's an easygoing guy with an innocuous agenda. So innocuous, we kept looking past him as a suspect. We've looked so far past him, we didn't even interview him when we should have." I pulled my phone from my pocket. "If Oscar is behind this, he can't find out about Bitsy." I groaned. "And we need to get in touch with that maid. If she isn't already in danger, she will be if Oscar thinks we suspect him. She had to be the one who sent the text from Blaine's phone."

Alex rubbed his neck. "He shouldn't have been able to deflect suspicion away from himself in such a broad way. He's too young to have that kind of power." He pulled his phone from his pocket. "I'll let Cornelius know, and see if he has some way to protect himself and Francis against whatever it is that Oscar's done to ramp-up his gifts."

Illusion and persuasion were both more difficult to maintain in the face of facts incongruous with the magical fiction. With hard evidence—or at least some evidence—against Oscar, maybe we could put a dent in some of the smoke-and-mirrors magic he was using. Assuming it really was Oscar.

Nuts. Whatever he was doing, he was good. Doubts were running around in my head like nasty little gremlins.

I called my surest bet for decent data, and he picked up after one ring. "Bradley! Please tell me you've found something, anything, on Oscar Hayes."

"I was about to call you. Not Oscar, Bitsy. Four payments from Bitsy's account to Tabitha's, every Friday over the last month."

"But nothing on Oscar?"

"Tabitha was the victim. They found her in Bitsy's car."

"Yes," I agreed. But I wanted dirt on Oscar.

I squeezed my eyes shut. Whether it was my debatable precog skills or just my old-fashioned inductive reasoning at work again, a vivid image of Bitsy's plain, bare-bones apartment popped into my head. No evidence of spare cash for bribes in that apartment. And Bitsy had only recently been bound to the killer.

I opened my eyes and smiled. "Exactly how much were those payments?"

Bradley named a figure that made my eyes pop, and I used to make a pretty decent living when I was still one hundred percent human.

"So tell me, Bradley, how hard would it have been for someone to plant that information in Bitsy's banking records?"

"I could do it."

In Bradley-speak, that meant difficult but doable. I was about to do a fist pump, but stopped when I saw Alex. He was standing in the middle of the living room, looking a lot like things weren't going well. *Focus, Mallory.* I cleared my throat and said, "Sorry, Bradley. Any way to prove that's what happened?"

"Yes, if that's what happened. I can't calculate how long it will take to find evidence."

"Well, do your best. And you know Bitsy makes a living as a waitress and is newly turned, so she probably doesn't have a bunch of cash stashed unless it's from family or another job we don't know about. Also, she hasn't been herself for the last four days. Anything done in that time period is suspect. And our chief suspect is Oscar Hayes. Blaine Waldrup is a close second. Be sure to check if the money ties to either of them." I stopped, took a breath, rubbed my chest, and said, "You know all this already."

"I do. "

"You probably want to get back to work."

"Yes."

When I finally hung up, Alex was missing. "Alex?"

"In the bedroom."

It was a small apartment, so there was only the kitchen, living room, bedroom, and one bathroom. I walked through the living room and joined him in the bedroom.

"Boone, get off the bed."

Boone rolled over on his side without looking at me. That short trail he'd run had worn him out more than I realized.

Alex shrugged. He cleared his throat and then said, "I already tried. She'll just have to wash the duvet cover—if she comes home."

I was trying hard not to worry about things I couldn't change, so I didn't linger over the unpleasant reminder that Bitsy's well-being was far from guaranteed at this point. Just thinking about it, made my chest hurt and I coughed.

"Have you found anything? Oh, please tell me there's no blood in the kitchen fridge."

"If there was, Francis or one of the emergency response team would have cleaned it out when they picked up Bitsy earlier." Alex shoved a nightstand drawer closed. "And there's nothing here but maybe two weeks of clothes and basic toiletries. Are we sure she didn't live somewhere else?"

My phone pinged with a text. I glanced down and saw it was from Bradley. That was fast, even for him.

A flicker of light in my peripheral vision caught my attention, but when I turned there was nothing there. And now I was hallucinating. Just dandy. I covered my mouth with the back of my hand and opened the text.

Found buried connection between O.H. and Bitsy while working on bank info. O.H. owns Bitsy's apartment complex.

A deep sense of dread filled me. Again, flickering light appeared at the edge of my vision.

"Alex?" I looked around the apartment, but nothing looked out of place. Still that sense of dread persisted. "Alex, I think we should leave. Boone!"

His body, sprawled on the bed, didn't move.

I couldn't catch my breath, which turned my worry to anger. Now was not the time for a very human anxiety attack. I rushed to the bed calling Boone's name. I tapped him on the shoulder. The sound of his name, my touch, nothing roused him. "Alex, he's not moving. Something's wrong."

The tightness in my chest grew, and again I felt the flash of dread.

And then I caught a picture. It was like a frame in a film, frozen for just an instant, and then gone again.

But that one frame was enough.

I screamed, "Alex!"

In that still life, I didn't see the room, the bed, the sleeping dog, Alex rummaging in the drawers. I saw smoke and flames.

21

NINJAS AND KARATE KICKS

Alex spun around at the sound of his name. "What?"

I tried to stay calm, because everything around us looked normal—except for Boone. He was still lying prone on the bed.

"Are you having any difficulty breathing?" I kept the tone of my voice even. Hard to do after having a nightmarish vision and screaming in panic.

"No." He looked at me oddly. "What's wrong?

My eyes were starting to tear. "Are you sure?" He tilted his head, so I repeated the question. "You're certain that you're not having any difficulties breathing?"

He frowned. Then he coughed. And when he started, he couldn't stop.

The tightness in my chest increased. I grabbed Alex by the arm. "We have to get out. The apartment is on fire."

"No..." Even as he choked out the word, he was denying the reality around him.

I dragged Alex by the arm to the bed and pointed to Boone's apparently sleeping form. "Pick him up. We have to go *now*."

Thank God Alex complied, because my supercharged vamp strength, agility, and speed were nowhere in sight.

I was going to kill Oscar, if all three of us made it out alive. If anything happened to Alex, or if—I gasped for breath. If Boone wasn't just sleeping, I was going to torture him first and then kill him.

Reality flashed for an instant, and I pulled on Alex's arm to stop him before he walked into a wall. I pointed. "Wall."

We'd just made a circle. Somehow, Oscar had trapped us inside a tiny, ground floor apartment with at least three possible exits.

"Which way?" Alex asked. His words sounded choked to my ears, but he looked fine.

"I don't know. We have to break the illusion. He's spinning us around in circles." I was pretty sure Alex and I wouldn't die from smoke inhalation, but Boone might. I didn't understand the effects of Celia's magic, didn't know what could kill him only that he healed faster than a normal dog.

A band tightened around my chest, and my eyes burned. Panic? Smoke?

I screamed in frustration.

"Hey, hey. Stop. Think." Alex bumped his arm against me. "I can only see the illusion, but you're seeing pieces. Put the reality together, and you break the illusion. Right?"

That was one option.

I screamed again, but this time it was for Tangwystl.

The ache in my chest eased when she appeared in my hand. I removed her from her scabbard, and slung it over my back. "How good are you at cutting through walls?"

Yuck.

Hearing her voice in my head made me laugh hysterically. Mostly because she was real, but also because I'd known she would hate this.

Alex gritted his teeth. "Please tell me she said she'd do it."

I let her slice through the air once. "I'm in a pinch. Can you do it...or are walls too hard for you?"

She squealed with indignation.

"That's what I thought."

Then she blew a raspberry.

"Put your hand on my back, Alex, so I don't I accidentally chop something important off." Then I started slashing.

After a few false starts, Tangwystl realized I couldn't see where I was going, and, Lord love her, she started to direct me.

Left, left, left, left, stabby-stab.

I hesitated and then thrust the blade into what looked like the air. It met with resistance, but it felt like cutting into butter.

Slice and dice.

I figured that meant I could cut an exit. As I moved the blade in a roughly door-shaped pattern, the etched symbols on her glowed and the resistance Tangwystl met, lessened. I had never been so happy to have a magical, sentient sword.

"That's our way out?" Alex sounded skeptical, but he also wasn't looking so hot. What I could see of him through the smoke.

I flinched as reality exploded into the illusion. "Oh my God." I choked on the words as I inhaled smoke.

Flames were all around us. Tangwystl, bless her, had found us a way out through the bathroom's exterior wall, the only room that wasn't engulfed in flames. I could see a rough, hole-shaped outline where I'd cut through the wall, but the cut-out portion hadn't fallen away.

Karate kick. Ninja.

But Alex beat me too it. With Boone cradled close to his chest, he gave the wall a solid kick. We'd both gathered enough pieces of reality to bust through the illusion.

A portion of the wall fell away, and without a backward glance Alex ducked through the opening.

I followed behind him and emerged to find a scene of complete chaos. Fire trucks, fireman, squad cars, residents —add the flashing lights and water and it was a circus. I took a few more steps, drew a few breaths of relatively clean air, and then realized that this was no circus. The flickering emergency lights amplified the impression of chaos, but everyone on this side of the barricade was moving in a controlled, even choreographed way.

I looked for Alex and found him moving toward the barricade. He stopped and turned around. "Call Wembley. Boone needs a vet—now."

I stood in the middle of all that movement, all those people, with a drawn blade in my hand. Not a single one of them saw me.

The illusion was still partially intact.

I sheathed Tangwystl and whispered, "You're the best sword. I promise we'll practice lots this week."

Promise, promise, promise, never practice.

"I will, but no more late night TV with Wembley. The ninjas and karate kicks gave you away."

She blew a raspberry at me.

My sword was getting cheekier by the day.

As I pulled out my phone, I saw a paramedic approach Alex. He'd either passed the illusion's perimeter or busted it entirely. I was about to call Wembley, but stopped when I saw him in the crowd. I shifted Tangwystl closer to my body and then sprinted towards Wembley.

I was about ten feet away when he saw me. "Mallory?"

"Yes. Alex has Boone and we need to get him to a vet. Do you have your van? Alex's car is blocked in the parking lot."

He gestured for me to follow. "I came as soon as Bradley told me Oscar owned the apartment complex you were planning to search."

"If you weren't in a hurry to get to your van, I'd hug you right now."

With both Wembley and I keeping an eye out for Alex and Boone, I'm not sure how we missed them but they beat us to the van. We were several feet from the Vanagon, when I spotted them. Alex was sitting on the ground, propped against a tire, and Boone was on the ground next to him. He looked like a puddle of red fur. He wasn't moving, and I couldn't see him breathing.

I thought my heart was going to break.

Then he lifted his head and gave me one of his classic mournful looks.

"Hey, watch it." Wembley stuffed a crisply folded hanky in my hand. "You're crying."

"Nuts." Just what I needed right now, a bunch of acid tear track marks on my face. I dabbed at the corners of my eyes. "Thanks, Wembley."

Alex stood up, then helped a wobbly Boone to his feet. "As soon as you started to cut through the wall, the illusion busted. I wasn't sure if Boone was still breathing, so I got him out of the smoke as fast as I could."

"You made the right choice. I spotted Wembley, and by the time I'd chased him down, you were nowhere in sight."

Wembley unlocked and opened the van's side door. "Boone's looking a little rough."

Alex steadied Boone as he stepped up into the van, and then gave the hound a boost to get him all the way in. "Yeah, he woke up almost immediately. He's actually recovering so quickly, I'm not sure we *can* take him to a vet."

Boone groaned.

I hopped in the back to sit with Alex and Boone, while Wembley climbed into the driver's seat.

"Are we taking him home then?" Wembley asked.

"Yeah," Alex replied. "Bradley's going to monitor him and take him to the emergency vet if he doesn't continue to improve."

Boone groaned again, but I wasn't sure if it was the possibility of a vet visit or the inevitability of an evening with Bradley.

"Before you got back," Alex said to me, "he wasn't this vocal. I kept talking to him, but no luck. He still only seems to understand when you're around."

Which had been a hidden blessing for me. A valuable investigative asset like Boone would otherwise have been given to a more qualified person, I was sure.

I moved so I could cradle his head in my lap, and I rubbed his ears. "I'm glad you're okay, buddy."

Boone groaned again, but this time it was in satisfaction.

"What exactly are we all doing that Bradley needs to take care of Boone?" Wembley left out the part about Bradley being particularly troubled by Boone's saliva, dander, and hair, and therefore not the most ideal of candidates.

"We're going to take care of a little pest problem," Alex said.

"Please tell me you have a plan, because I'm so tired." I yawned widely enough to crack my jaw. "Excuse me. Ever since Bitsy used me as a buffet, I've been a little tired.

Anyway, I'm not sure my brain is working well enough to formulate a plan for dinner, let alone one to overthrow a master illusionist's grand plan for world domination."

Wembley whistled. "I think I've missed some important parts of this story."

"Oh, I have a plan," Alex said. "As to what you've missed…"

22

SINGING SWORDS AND SWINGING SWORDS

"Mallory."

"Hmmm." My lips were dry and my mouth felt like cotton.

Someone shook my shoulder, and then a horn blared.

"What?" I jerked awake.

"Was that necessary, Wembley?" Alex asked. He leaned into the van and eyed me critically. "You need some water."

Wembley tapped the horn again, but lightly this time. "Absolutely necessary. Let's get a move on, people. Adventure awaits." A bottle of water came flying from the front seat of Wembley's van.

Alex caught it, twisted the cap off, and handed it to me. "We dropped off Boone with Bradley, and we're in the parking lot of Bits, Baubles, and Toadstools now. We're heading in to meet with Cornelius, check on Bitsy, and then have a chat with Blaine's maid, Rosa."

I guzzled half the bottle. "Right. Wait—the maid, the one who we thought Oscar might try to target, her name is Rosa?" Something about that bothered me.

"Finish your water," Wembley said as he handed me a second one. "Alex is right, you need serious hydration. You're looking parched."

I finished the rest of the first bottle, and then got out of the van with the second tucked under my arm.

Alex was hovering over me like I was an invalid one second and then the next second, time stopped.

Not stopped, slowed to an impossible crawl. Good thing, because otherwise, I might not have been fast enough to stop Alex from slicing Oscar in half.

It was also a good thing I'd squeezed in a little snooze or my vampy superspeed might not have kicked in. Turned out, time hadn't slowed, I'd just sped up that much.

I had no recollection of moving from the van to a point twenty feet away, but I was there, Alex was there, and Oscar was there. Some part of my brain must have seen Alex draw his sword. I can't imagine what else would have kicked in my superspeed.

Vamp speed—when it occasionally worked for me— rocked. I drew Tangwystl and blocked the strike meant for the unarmed Oscar.

Alex immediately stepped back, his sword raised in a defensive position.

I sheathed Tangwystl, who was singing a happy tune over being drawn again so soon, but I stayed firmly planted between Oscar and Alex.

From behind me, Oscar said in a small voice, "Is your sword singing?"

Alex took another step back and sheathed his sword. Normally, it disappeared from sight, but it remained conspicuously present. "I don't suppose you'd like explain why he's still breathing."

"Ah," I said, scrambling for the answer. "Excellent question." Especially since I'd wanted to kill him myself not so long ago. But Alex typically had a cool head. Something had him all sorts of pissed off. Oh, yes, Boone and I almost dying. Yep, that would piss off Alex, Mr. Protector himself.

Oscar cleared his throat. "If I can—"

"No," Alex said.

Maintaining eye contact with Alex, I took a teensy step to the right. When he didn't draw his sword, I took another, slightly larger step. Maintaining eye contact, I moved just enough so that I can look from one to the other. "Wembley?" I called out.

"He can't hear you. He's inside, retrieving something to protect us from his illusions." Alex was watching me carefully. "I hope he hurries, because I'm half convinced you're in the midst of one."

Oscar took a step forward. "No, in fact—"

I shushed Oscar, but Alex had already drawn his sword.

"Oscar, do you *want* to lose your head?" I frowned at Alex. "I am not drawing my sword again, not against you, but you are not lopping his head off without more information."

A strangled sound emerged from Oscar's lips, but the man had enough sense to shut the heck up.

I tuned out Tangwystl's protestations over remaining sheathed and considered whether I was more concerned for Oscar or for Alex. No, scratch that. Definitely Alex. He carried around guilt like some precious thing he couldn't let go of. Killing Oscar without definitive proof would be a terrible burden, as soon as his sense of justice and fair play came crawling back. And they would any minute now.

When I gave Alex a testy look, he relaxed slightly and sheathed his sword, but it's visible presence was a reminder that head lopping might still happen.

I pointed at Oscar. "Yes or no, are you casting an illusion right now?"

"No."

Alex snorted. "You believe him?"

"Yeah, I do." I said it regretfully, because I felt like a ninny. *Sure, I believe the illusionist con-artist guy.* How could I not feel like an ass? I reached inside, looking for that spark of precognition that Wembley swore I had—but I pulled up a big fat nothing. Which prompted me to use my words. "Why *are* you here, Oscar?"

I sent him a look that said, "make it good, buddy." Superfluous given the presence of Alex and his sword, but given how close I'd come to being immolated I figured I was allowed a little attitude.

A look of mingled frustration and anger crossed his face. "To withdraw from the selection."

"Ohhhh," I nodded like I had a clue why our prime suspect would be neutralizing his primary motive for committing all his crimes.

I had no clue. Not one.

Oscar picked up on that, because he said, "I didn't like the direction the nominations were taking. With Blaine as the only candidate, and his platform so clearly, ah—" He glanced at me. "No offense, but his platform is blatantly vampire-oriented, old-school vampire. Given the direction the Society has been moving, the positive changes that have been happening, that seemed wrong. And I felt obligated to do something to make it right."

"Obligated?" I glanced at Alex, but he looked equally confused. "I don't get it. Why you? You're hardly involved with the Society. You don't even live in town."

Oscar ran a hand through his hair. "My family has deep

ties to the region. But now I'm not sure *I* wasn't manipulated to take the nomination."

Alex swore. "You were one of the ousted families." His voice was firm, certain. Dang it. I should have listened to that big lecture on the founding families.

Families. A light bulb turned on in my head.

"Oh, my." Family was the key. Who else but a coyote could wield illusion? Other coyotes. And Cornelius or Alex had said that Oscar wasn't strong enough—wasn't *old* enough—to work some of the magic we'd encountered. And who would be so ambitious for a family member? Someone older, a father, a mother.

Oscar truly wasn't responsible for the fire, or Tabitha, or even Bitsy. I was most disturbed by Bitsy's treatment. More so than a murder, which was troubling. Maybe I'd been spending so much time with Alex that his aversion to persuasion had permeated my subconscious. And Bitsy had been under a greater influence than persuasion. She'd been a puppet in her own body.

A wash of sympathy for Oscar flooded me. Those terrible things were all done ostensibly for his benefit. "You didn't have anything to do with Bitsy, with any of it."

His nostrils pinched with anger, but he didn't say anything. He wouldn't, not if the person responsible was his family.

I started to ask Oscar who, even though I knew he wouldn't say, but Alex said, "Rosa. She had access to Blaine's phone and to Bitsy before her disappearance."

And that was why Alex didn't take notes but I should.

"I don't suppose you know a very pretty maid named Rosa, aka Rosa Silver, who also happens to be a member of the Divorced Diva's club?"

He looked stymied. "Divorced Divas? What in the—" His

lips pinched together and he shook his head. "I'm fairly certain Rosa, Blaine's maid, is my grandmother. I don't know about this Divorced Divas club."

"Your grandmother?" Alex turned his gaze to a point behind my back. "Any chance you can keep your grandmother's illusions under control? I think she might be headed this way."

23

SKULLDUGGERY REVEALED

I spun around, ready to face the sickly, rot-ridden apple of this case: Grandma Rosa. Except there was no petite dark-haired maid.

Why would there be? That young woman couldn't be Oscar's grandmother. She was much too young. Illusion, persuasion, manipulation. Grandma Rosa was a master, so naturally she would have assumed a disguise. If I had to guess, I'd say Bitsy was particularly susceptible to young, petite, pretty, dark-headed women.

The woman who approached was not that girl.

Elegant, that was the first word that came to mind. Rosa, if that was even her name, was a timeless beauty. High round cheekbones, midnight hair swept up into a simple but attractive style, flawless skin that was neither youthful nor lined, and her clothing was beautifully tailored. She could have been thirty-five or fifty if she was human.

The woman who was apparently Oscar's grandmother was escorted by none other than Cornelius. She let go of his arm, but not before she gave him a fond pat.

"Nana," Oscar said. Disappointment and exhaustion clouded his voice.

"Please, Oscar. If they're going to exile me, the least you can do is call me Grandmother. You know I can't abide that name." She turned to smile at Alex. "My grandson is not capable of 'keeping my illusions in check,' but I've promised Mr. Lemann to be on my very best behavior, and in exchange he has agreed to allow my grandson to continue with the selection."

"No." Oscar's face tensed. In a firmer voice he said again, "No."

A motorcycle zoomed by, and I realized we were having a pretty darn frank conversation about Society business *in the parking lot*. Forget all the casual sword waving that had already happened. "Ah," I raised my hand. "Excuse me."

Cornelius, with no attempt to hide his exasperation, said, "Yes, Ms. Andrews."

"Should we maybe go inside to have this conversation?" I winced when Cornelius turned his evil, laser beam eyes on me. I hated when he did that. Sure, his gaze didn't actual cut me, but the glow of his evil laser eyes always made me feel like he could slice and dice his way down to my very soul.

"No, we will not be going inside. Lucinda, Ms. Hayes, was just leaving. I'm escorting her to the airport myself." He shifted his gaze from me to Lucinda Hayes. "We've concluded our negotiations, and she will be leaving the United States immediately."

"I'm terribly sorry for the inconvenience at the apartment complex, Oscar." He gave her a confused look, and she inclined her head. "Oh, you don't know. I'm afraid it's suffered rather extensive fire damage. I put that particular trick in place before I knew the whole house of cards was falling. I'll make sure you're reimbursed."

Oscar closed his eyes. I could almost see him counting to ten. When he opened them, he only said, "Was anyone hurt?"

"No, not that I've been made aware. These two were the intended targets, and they've clearly made their way to safety." Her tone was accusatory, as if we'd inconvenienced her by not dying as intended in the fire.

"But the others, they were you, weren't they, Nana?"

She closed her eyes and raised her eyebrows at the use of the ill-favored name.

"You killed that woman, didn't you, Grandmother?"

"Well, no. Not exactly." She considered her answer, and then said, "Perhaps a very little bit. But it was the vampire who struck the fatal blow."

And everyone said vampires were sociopaths. I snapped my mouth shut. I would not gape. On reflection, I wasn't sure if the fine slicing of blame fell into sociopath territory or was more narcissism. Or just flat out delusional toddler syndrome: I want what I want and I don't care who I hurt.

"And Bitsy?" I asked, trying to keep the bitchy in my voice to a minimum. "What did you do to her?"

"I've already explained to Cornelius." I nailed her with a nasty look, and when Cornelius didn't leap to her defense, she said, "She should have died, but Cornelius has explained that she's going to recover. She'll have all sorts of incriminating memories, so here I am." She lifted both hands. "Confessing, negotiating, conceding—just like old times. Except back then, the escort out of town wasn't nearly so charming." She smiled at Cornelius.

Anton's Escalade pulled up.

No way. She wasn't disappearing into thin air without explaining herself. I grabbed a question from the ether. "The blood test said you weren't immune."

"Did it?" She smiled. "Did it really say that?"

"The text to Gladys." She started to leave, and without thinking twice, I drew Tangwystl. "The text?"

Cornelius's eyes blazed, but Lucinda placed a hand on his arm. "I sent the text. I set the fire. I bound the woman. I fed the stone to the assistant. Anything else?"

"The stones," I said. Granted, the root of all evil here was Lucinda, but those stones had played a huge part in several unsavory plots.

Cornelius's patience, already thin, snapped. "Enough."

His voice low and just a little scary, Alex said, "I don't think so. Where are the stones?"

"Recovered, most of them." He sighed. "And safe for now."

"How did she come upon them?" Alex asked.

Which was a rocking question, because I had a bad feeling about that. They'd done serious damage, both in death count and to the Society in general. Indirectly, true, but the stones had landed with people who had malice in their hearts. They couldn't be a coincidence.

"*She*," Lucinda said, "was given them as a gift by an admirer. Nothing nefarious there, I assure you. I scattered them locally using a displacement spell with the intent of stirring up a little chaos and discord." She raised her eyebrows. "There might be a few small stones missing from the set. You'll have to reassemble it to find out. I can't remember exactly how many I set loose into the wild."

As my brain scrambled for those unanswered questions I knew I'd later regret not asking, Cornelius whisked her inside Anton's SUV.

At some point, Anton had quietly exited the SUV. He'd waited and watched and listened—I'm not sure for how long. But before he returned to the driver's seat, I saw the look on his face. He was as disgusted as I was.

Our eyes met, and we shared a very brief moment of mutual agreement. Mean Mr. Clean and I were never on the same page. Then he climbed into his SUV, and I was left to wonder if I'd imagined it.

Cornelius turned to us with his hand on the passenger door. "Oscar, your grandmother has negotiated your right to remain in the selection. You have until Friday to decide whether you wish to accept or decline the nomination."

He tipped his head at us and then climbed into the passenger seat of the Escalade.

I stared as the Escalade departed. Inside was a nasty piece of work who'd heartlessly turned several lives upside down in pursuit of her own selfish ends, and she wasn't in chains. She wasn't headed for a witch-enchanted noose.

Lucinda Hayes was headed to an island paradise. Or maybe a Scottish castle or an igloo in a cold clime.

The point was, she was off to a new and most likely prison-free life, and I was left feeling like a naïve, silly little girl for thinking that just wasn't fair.

24

THE MYSTERIOUS WAYS OF SOCIETY JUSTICE

"**W**hat did I miss?" Wembley looked from Alex, to me, to Oscar.

And we probably all looked shell-shocked.

"I saw Anton leave with Cornelius and some woman. Alex's sword isn't shoved in this guy's throat. And you look like someone stole your last vegan shake."

Oscar didn't even blink when Wembley alluded to the possibility of his jugular being opened up. I figured that last part was aimed at me, being the only vegan in the group, but like Oscar, I was just too done with the whole situation to even respond.

Maybe it was shock. Maybe blood loss from Bitsy's snack. But probably disappointment. The world had let me down. My world, anyway.

Alex put his arm around my shoulders. "You need a drink."

Wembley threw his hands up in the air. "I'm guessing I can leave my sword in the van, since this guy"—he hitched a thumb at Oscar—"doesn't seem to be the bad guy."

"It was my grandmother." And then Oscar filled Wembley in on the details.

I just huddled against Alex and listened. I did need a drink, but I didn't want to move. I didn't want to lose the comfort of Alex's arm wrapped around me.

"Oh, Mallory." Wembley shook his head. "You've just seen big enhanced politics at work. "Oscar, your grand-mother was an original founding member of Austin's governing body, wasn't she? Not just part of the family."

Oscar nodded.

I could feel a grumble discontent building in my chest. "She has a get-out-of-jail-free card—even for murder—because she was a founding member of Austin's original enhanced governing body?"

"She didn't murder anyone, not technically," Oscar reminded me. "And even if you consider attenuated actions and intent, the greater offense was to leave a visibly bitten body for humans to find. The Society has always viewed reveal scandals harshly. Her attacks on you, Mallory, Alex, that was merely politics in her mind, and just a few steps away from a feud or duel."

"And Bitsy?" Alex's voice was barely more than a whisper. "There is no excuse for—"

"No. But neither is there any excuse for her other actions," Oscar said. "What she did, everything she did, was reprehensible, but she's not so careless as she might appear."

"So according to the Society, in engineering a death, she became less culpable than the tools she used?" My mind spun at the thought. "Blaine was a tool, and whoever picked up and redeposited Tabitha's body in the parking lot. And Bitsy, if she somehow got Tabitha to eat that amethyst." My vision narrowed, and I just knew that my eyes were bleeding red. "Bitsy... What your grandmother did to her..." Words failed me.

"I agree. I can't say that I wish her to be executed. She's my grandmother. But I do wish there was something beyond exile to be done. Something that might dissuade future, equally reprehensible acts." Oscar ran his hand through his already mussed hair. "She's a ruthless woman."

His arm still tucking me snugly against his side, Alex said, "I gather she used some type of persuasion to keep us from either suspecting you or noticing her involvement?"

"Undoubtedly," Oscar said. "That's well beyond my skill. She has a great deal of power, exceptional control, and she's lived long enough to have gathered together a vast store of practical magical knowledge. All of that makes her dangerous. Add to that her single-mindedness when pursuing a goal, and she's a force to be reckoned with. I wish I'd understood how much she wanted this position for me. Maybe if I'd known..."

But really, what could he have done? Alone, without help from the Society, I suspected very little. And then he'd have been responsible for turning his own grandmother in without any real proof.

Oscar rubbed his face. "I keep hoping that we're outgrowing our past, leaving exactly this type of entitlement and corruption behind."

Which sounded suspiciously like my own hopes for the Society. "You're sure you don't want to be the next CEO?"

Oscar let loose a mirthless laugh. "I only ever planned to accept the nomination because the alternative was Blaine. He's an outright bigot. I'm fond of Austin. It's my hometown. And to think of that backward idiot running the Society, it makes me heartsick. Blaine was exceptional motivation for me to run." He shook his head. "Nana likely guaranteed Blaine's participation in the selection for just that reason. I can't believe I didn't suspect the depth of her involvement."

He needed to stop speaking, because the more he said, the more I liked him. I did *not* want to like the man whose grandma just about broiled me, my partner, and my hound. I couldn't even think about poor Bitsy. I could only imagine what heinous things she'd had to do under Nana's control.

"I'm not interested in accepting the nomination." Alex said. Looking at Oscar, he added, "In case you were considering withdrawing."

"You need to accept, Alex. For the good of the Society. I'm done with it all. My crazy family, the selection, even Austin. I'm moving as soon as I find out where my nutjob nana lands." Oscar winced. "I'm not taking the chance of landing in her backyard."

And that did it. The man recognized crazy when he saw it, didn't have a problem with humans, and seemed to have some sense of justice. He needed to be the new CEO. "You need to stay. And someone needs to take care of that ridiculous excuse for a candidate, Blaine Waldrup." I gave Wembley a speculative look. "Are you sure you don't have some of those Berserker drugs stashed away?"

Wembley rolled his eyes. "Be glad I rediscovered my sense of humor last century. Also, that would be interfering with the selection. You want me shipped off like Lucinda? Exiled from Austin for the foreseeable future?"

I huffed out an annoyed breath and mumbled, "No."

Alex extended his hand to Oscar and said, "Stay."

Oscar lost the bland used car salesman look that had clung to him. And I'd swear he stood a little taller when he grasped Alex's hand. He didn't say anything, just nodded once.

After Oscar had climbed into his practical white Honda to drive to his home in the suburbs, I was even more certain he was exactly what the Society needed. Looking at Alex, I said, "That means he's in, right? That we're not going to be stuck with Blaine?"

"I think it means he's going to try."

A tiny bud of hope unfurled in my chest. Sure, I was still royally pissed that Lucinda Hayes had gone free, and I was very disappointed that she was getting a new life rather than a prison sentence. But maybe things within the Society would be better tomorrow. And if not tomorrow, maybe the day after that. With someone like Oscar Hayes as our possible future leader, maybe a little hope was okay.

"And if he doesn't win, we can bury Blaine in a deep pit someplace where no one will ever find him." I grinned at Alex and Wembley.

Wembley laughed. "That's my girl." He hooked arms with me, and I hooked arms with Alex, and then the three of us headed back to the van.

"You look like you could use a good night's sleep," Alex said.

"Always with the flattery. Thanks, Alex." I climbed into Wembley's Vanagon. "No time for sleep, guys. Tonight's bingo night at the senior center, and we're Bradley's backup. Besides, you don't want to miss meeting Dot the bingo-playing, dark-web-cruising, hacker grandma, do you?"

We were all agreed that bingo night was a must-attend, and Dot was a must-not-miss.

So I entertained myself with images of hacking grandmothers and mega bingo wins on the ride home, while I absently picked at the scabbed over bit marks on my arm.

To read more about Bradley's adventures at bingo night, pick up the next Vegan Vamp book, The Halloween Haunting!

BONUS CONTENT

Interested in bonus content for the Vegan Vamp series? Subscribe to my newsletter to receive a bonus chapter for *Adventures of a Vegan Vamp* as well as release announcements and other goodies! Sign up at http://eepurl.com/b6pNQP.

ABOUT THE AUTHOR

Cate Lawley is the pen name for Kate Baray's sweet romances and cozy mysteries, including The Goode Witch Matchmaker and Vegan Vamp series. When she's not tapping away at her keyboard or in deep contemplation of her next fanciful writing project, she's sweeping up hairy dust bunnies and watching British mysteries with her pointers and hounds.

Cate also writes urban and paranormal fantasy as Kate Baray and thrillers as K.D. Baray.

For more information:
www.catelawley.com
www.facebook.com/katebaray
www.twitter.com/katebarayauthor

Printed in Great Britain
by Amazon

18909112R00119